14

P9-DEP-971

THE

FARM

SHE

WAS

THE
FARM
SHE
WAS

a novel

WITHDRAWN

Croton Free Library
CROTON-ON-HUDSON
NEW YORK 10520

Ann Mohin

Bridge Works Publishing Co.
Bridgehampton, New York

Copyright © 1998
All rights reserved under International and Pan-American
Copyright Conventions.

Published in 1998 in the United States by Bridge Works
Publishing Company, Bridgehampton, New York.
Distributed in the United States by National Book Network,
Lanham, Maryland.

First Edition

The characters and events in this book are fictitious. Any
similarity to actual persons, living or dead, is coincidental and
not intended by the author.

Library of Congress Cataloging-in-Publication Data

Mohin, Ann,
    The farm she was : a novel / Ann Mohin. — 1st ed.
        p.   cm.
    ISBN 1-882593-21-9 (hc : alk. paper)
    I. Title.
    PS3563.0343F37   1998
    813′.54 — dc21   97-42255

10   9   8   7   6   5   4   3   2   1

Book and jacket design by Eva Auchincloss
Jacket Illustration by Eva Auchincloss

Printed in the United States of America

AP 28 '98

———•••——— ———•••——— ———•••——— ———•••———

For my husband Bill
and in memory of my father,
Edward J. Purcell (1900–1981)

———•••——— ———•••——— ———•••——— ———•••———

With gratitude to Barbara Block, Bruce Coville, Jane Driscoll, Sue Ferrara, Mark Garland, Bill Metzger and Marie Summerwood for their constant reassurance and support.

Special thanks to Barbara and Warren Phillips and Billie Fitzpatrick, whose editorial assistance and enthusiasm are so greatly appreciated.

Finally, I am deeply grateful to Andrea and Tim Mohin for caring, as well as to my mother, Josephine Purcell, for never doubting, not once.

The
Farm
She
Was

Chapter One

IN CENTRAL NEW YORK SPRING UNFOLDS as slowly as the fiddlehead ferns that lay a pale green carpet on the floor of the woods. The relentless white of January and February suffocates optimism, and the disappointing sleet and mud of March and April threaten a person's confidence.

I know this is true, for all of my seasons have passed here in this unsympathetic region, all of my years on this sheep farm, my home. It is here, in this farmhouse on Pike Road in the town of Donohue Flats, that I was born ninety years ago. It is here — I hope on a warm and sunny day — that I expect to die. Not now, not in May, when cheerful birds build their nests and daffodils bob their heads above the pliant ground, but soon.

Esther shushes me when I say things like that. I'm her Social Services assignment and what a tough one I must be. What with these locked-up bones, I can hardly get out of my bed. She is not a full-fledged nurse, but she gives me my medication and bathes

1

this pink crepe paper called skin. She cooks my breakfast and sweeps my floor just as spotlessly as she would her own, and before she leaves each day she sits next to this bed, which has been moved for purposes of convenience into the parlor, and reads me *The Evening Star.*

So here I am, living in the house where I was born, waiting for patient Esther to tend my needs. My lifeline is dangerously frayed, but my mind is sharper than a cat's eye; I remember. Though my body is brittle and dry, my vision is clear, and my ears, trying hard to hear, wiggle and twitch. But my own voice has betrayed me. Once a melodiously sculpted soprano, it is now no more beautiful than the cackle of an old hen.

Still, Esther listens to these rambles, these little memories I've jotted down in this journal, the few stories I am willing to share. And she talks to me. Lately though, she's been saying things I don't like to hear, things about the Pine Manor Home over in Wichner and how much easier my life would be there.

Esther is golden.

She says, "I worry about you, Miss Leahy, alone all night long. What if something goes wrong?"

The camera of an old woman's mind shoots from many angles.

"Joe will bark," I answer, knowing full well that the old border collie has all but lost the desire to bark and even if he did, no one would hear him. My nearest neighbor is half a mile away. "Just help me

2

into the bathroom every night before you leave." I laugh. "I don't plan on getting out of this bed," I lie, for that, sooner or later, is exactly what I plan to do.

I will go up the stairs to the attic, where buried in one of the neatly stacked cardboard boxes is a gift I want to give to Esther. Perhaps it will still her hands, which tremble over the layers of cream she massages into my skin. Perhaps it will brighten her sad eyes.

"You would be safer at Pine Manor," she tells me.

As if I would ever leave my farm.

Young women like Esther with two sweet children and a husband who works hard enough, but does, I suspect, take a long nip now and then, would claw the walls until their fingers were bloodied nubs before they would allow themselves to be stripped from their homes, transported to a warehouse like Pine Manor.

So, she should know, would a childless old spinster like me.

THIS FARMHOUSE WAS BUILT IN 1845 IN THE center of eighty-five, half-wooded rolling acres. It was a small and self-contained farm, but now its fields and pastures are fallow and overgrown. Damaged remnants of fieldstone fences limp through the trees — maple and cherry, oak and poplar, hemlock, beech, and the wild apples.

Rugged Germans first cleared this land, leveling the dense forest with two-man saws, pulling and burning the stumps with horses, plowing up fieldstones like bones in a cemetery. With hands for machines and back-breaking labor, they used those rocks to build four-foot high, geometrically-perfect fences. As proficient as trained masons, they selected each fieldstone like a poet selects her words. They laid the flat stones one atop the other for miles and miles through the woods until the cows and the sheep could, finally, be allowed to roam.

How did their muscles survive the labor, their skin the blistering sun? Their suffering will remind us of the past, forever — until bulldozers raid this land, obliterating the achievements of an era.

The man who built our house and cleared our fields and built the stone walls, certainly drove himself hard. Having completed his mission here in New York, he gathered his family and abandoned the state in 1859. My father's eyes sometimes glistened when he told the story of this German immigrant whose land and home we had acquired, how he packed up his belongings and moved to Ohio. There he cleared another piece of land, built another post-and-beam house, more stone walls.

I've always wondered why he left New York to start all over again. He had built a beautiful home, and the barns and the pastures and orchards were clear of rocks. Did he leave because of the hard weather? Or was it the acidic soil of this region where field crops are limited to cabbage and corn? Could it have been that he was simply bored?

The German had an engineer's mind. The house is sited precisely to benefit from the most southern sun and the high ridge to the north side protects against the killer winds. My father's building skills were comparatively limited, but his carpentry was adequate and the barns and wagons were not in disrepair. Father understood the meaning of maintenance, and to keep the farm in forward motion he adequately taught himself the art of reconstruction.

When Mother complained that the house was too dark, he put windows where there were none. The forest is visible from every room and now in May, when finally, finally, spring can be trusted to stay, new leaves accessorize my father's handiwork like lime-colored curtains and white tufts of the early flowers sway from tender shadbush branches. I stare out this window next to my bed and yes, I do remember other seasons, other times. The seasons are still intact; to hope for more than that is a foolish exertion.

THE WINTER OF 1911 HAD BEEN ICILY fierce, the worst I could remember. It was the first time in my eleven years that I recognized the wintry hazards stalking the unprepared. The hills across the valley, normally a clear view from our kitchen window, stayed obscurely gray, blanketed for months in dense, wet fog. Even the snow that fell that year seemed dark and heavy, and night after night the hot soapstone my mother tucked under my quilt was as cold as a block of ice by morning. But finally the wretched winter released its hold on the land and the waters of the great annual thaw could be heard advancing through the woods in a flood of defeat. Indisputable signs of the changing season were everywhere. The flocks of geese had already sailed up from the south, honking high above the fields in fluid patterns. The cherry trees toasted the woods, their leaf buds as promising and colorful as a glass of red wine. But not until the shadbushes bloomed did I begin to believe that it was safe to embrace spring.

The other sure sign that winter was defeated, the arrival of millions of small, black, flying insects, had already commenced. Some call them punkies, or mayflies, or black flies, or no-see-ums, but in our part of the county they're known as shadflies. They travel in clouds around an unprotected head, drilling bloody holes into its flesh. Farmers who repair fences in early May sport the badge of the spring season — itchy, angry red welts around the edge of their hats. Mother always said it showed God's sense of humor that the shadbush and the shadfly come out on exactly the same day of the month, but not a shadbush blooms that doesn't remind me of the evening Father invited me to go turkey hunting.

It's painted in glossy colors on my memory, for my father was a solitary man, and when he felt the need for a companion, he always chose his younger brother Alton. More than once my mother had asked him to take her for a walk in the woods surrounding our house. "Let's go down to the hemlocks tomorrow, like we used to," she would say. But tomorrow was always packed with other things to do and I can't remember them ever taking a walk together.

Father genuinely loved his brother, and so, as a result, did I. But the world seemed to baffle my Uncle Alton. His head sank deep between his shoulder blades as if he were trying to hide, and though he worked hard and steadily, his clothes never changed and his money was scarce.

Around the farm Uncle Alton was as common as a field mouse, but he rarely ate supper at our table, preferring, Father said, to go home. Home was above the livery in Donohue Flats, a few small rooms where he was free to play his fiddle, drink from an amber bottle, eat out of a pot. Primarily, it was a place free of the disapproving gaze of my mother, who never was able to see her brother-in-law's merits, no matter what he did to show them to her.

So it was more than a surprise when Father asked me, rather than my uncle, to go turkey hunting with him. He himself had not gone for years. According to my mother, he quit hunting the year that Billy died.

I was two and my brother was four when it happened. What I remember of that day has been bleached by time. In some osmosis of childish comprehension I knew that Billy was dead, though not

for many years did I know what killed him. I suppose I'd heard of the "summer complaint," a diag-
nostic phrase we used before penicillin was available.
Many people, and animals too, passed for want of
that miracle drug. But I would be a tall and gangly
teenager before I would learn that the medicine of
the century could not have saved my brother's life.
Only the Savior could have rescued the boy, and He
was apparently in no mood for children. But I'll hold
my tongue on that subject, lest my heathen thoughts
conjure up young Reverend Thorne again. That man
appears at my door with the regularity of a housefly,
and I have no desire to be pestered by him right now.

I still have one tintype of Billy and me sitting on
a velvet chair, me with ribbons in my sausage curls.
My baby legs are pudgy stumps peeking from under
a flowing dress. Billy looks sickly with large, indifferent eyes, and neither of us is smiling. He's buried
under an apple tree between Father and Mother on
the top of a hill overlooking the house. So is Molly,
my best sheep dog. I don't think I'll ever again walk
the hill to the Leahy cemetery, but I watch the roses
I planted there so many years ago like the guardian
I am.

From the window next to this bed I can see how
they are untended now, unpruned, overtaken with
burdocks and thistles and matted grass. Reverend
Thorne offered to tend the overgrown graves, but I
told him I had a gardener for such tasks. Of course
that is a lie, but the last thing I want is one of God's

men working for me. It's a hypocrite who calls on God when death is lurking at the foot of the bed. The man's presence makes me nervous; his kindness makes me wary.

That particular spring day when Father asked me to go turkey hunting had been a gift to us all after the unusually hard winter. Even the lines in Mother's face were smooth, the corners of her lips tipped up. It was after supper, and Father was in a good frame of mind. He leaned back in his chair, letting his right hand dangle almost to the floor to scratch Molly's pointy little ears.

"You make the best chicken and dumplings in the county, Ginny. Sure did hit the spot," he said, stroking his beard clean of crumbs.

I dallied awhile before clearing the table to bask in the pleasure of the cozy kitchen. Molly swung her black and white tail across the floor, mopping the same semicircle back and forth, back and forth, when all of a sudden Father sat up straight as a stick and clapped his hands hard. The dog bolted behind the cook stove. It sounded like a shot and I couldn't blame her for panicking. She wasn't gun-shy like some dogs, but she did jump out of her skin once in a while. For a minute even I thought something bad had happened. But Father was looking at Mother with a big, silly grin on his face, and his eyes flashed excitedly. Startled, she said too loudly, "William Leahy! What in the world is the matter with you?"

She probably thought it had something to do with her supper that had taken most of the day to fix. I knew because I was the one who killed the chicken.

"I just had a very good idea, Ginny." He made his eyes go big and round like silver dollars, and that fast they were smiling at each other again, though neither had the kind of teeth you might see in the Sears catalog. Father had taken a personal dislike to the new dentist in town, and my mother's smile was of the tight-lipped variety, so her dark and missing teeth were usually well hidden.

"Reeni," he practically yelled, "How about you and me going for a turkey tomorrow. You want to, girl? It's about time I showed my daughter a gobbler, and I heard one up above the house early this morning."

Well, Mother's face darkened the room like a window shade, and I wondered uneasily why Father didn't know better than to suggest such a thing. I rose to my feet slowly and Molly, magically sensing a storm, crept out of the room.

But he was the one who had opened this rabbit hutch and I wasn't about to close it. I knew exactly what my mother would have to say about her girl hunting turkeys or anything else. It was all right for me to clean a stall, slop a hog, or wring a chicken's neck, but my mother did not want me to carry a gun. "Too dangerous," she would say, gazing out the window at the tree tops on the other side of the pond. "Everything is too dangerous."

Still, I wanted to learn how to shoot more than anything else on earth. I had been reading about the wild west in school and for a whole year restricted my book reports to Annie Oakley and the Buffalo Girls. In the end, of course, I could shoot the eye out of a peacock, if I had to, but that was a skill I developed many years later. If I had the strength to hold up a shotgun now, I might still be able to hit a big tin can.

Mother pumped the dish water. Her hands were quite large but the grip had gone bad. She was not a small-boned woman and her muscles were unattractively bulky. Every morning she coiled a thick pale braid out of the way on the top of her head. I could not have known then that in twenty-five years I would resemble her so closely, that long after she was dead, my own reflection would suddenly bring tears of contrition and loss.

It was at this moment, on the eve of the adventure with my father, that I first saw my mother with what I would come to know later as the clear eyes of the wild turkey. The taste of how complicated it might be to grow into a woman dried my mouth.

The evening had taken a strange turn and the dishes remained dirty on the table while Father and I waited to hear what she might say. I pulled loose strings from the hem of my damp apron. Mother's was stained with the day. Its rusty color clashed with her faded yellow dress; its ruffle hung limp and flat.

Finally she turned away from the sink, put her hands on her hips and said, "William, for heaven's sake! There is no need for Irene to go turkey hunting."

His face fell down to the floor, and my eye started to twitch the way it still does to this day, when events warrant such a weakness.

"Ginny," he said softly, "she won't be carrying a gun. I'm just going to see if we can find a turkey, that's all. No gun."

Exasperated, she looked at him hard.

"Oh, all right. Get to bed early then," she surrendered. I tried to hug her, but she turned away and it was Molly who followed me up the stairs to my room.

Chapter Two

THE NEXT MORNING WHEN FATHER rapped on my door I was not sure whether the muffled voices I had heard the night before, rising and falling somewhere deep in the house, had been in my dream, but I believe now they were not, and that I did hear my mother softly crying. When I came downstairs about an hour before daybreak, a banquet of aromas drew me into the kitchen. Sausage and potatoes, eggs and coffee and toast with apple butter lay ready on the table. Mother had prepared a full breakfast for us though she did not speak a word till we slipped out the screen door.

"Don't slam it," she said quietly, partly out of habit and partly because a sharp noise would have destroyed the peace of dawn like the shot of a gun.

Early-morning stars peeked through the charcoal sky. The roosters throughout the valley roused each other and all around us songbirds stirred. We headed a quarter of a mile up Pike Road. Most people drag their feet on a dirt road, but I lifted my feet carefully and tried hard to preserve the natural sounds of the morning. Father did not have to try.

"Walk two steps, listen three steps," he whispered as we left the road for an old, well-traveled deer run.

The woods were wet with the May morning and the deeper we went, the more my feet turned into heavy weights, anchors I could not manage in the dense underbrush. Father, puzzled, stopped to look back at me, his finger to his lips.

I took two steps up a gentle incline toward him and stopped to listen. A branch cracked. Perhaps we had flushed a deer. Twisting too fast to look behind me, I noisily lost my balance. With an irritated wave of his hand, Father signaled to be quiet.

My heart raced. I wanted to show my father how I could walk through the woods, stealthy and sure-footed, just the right way to find turkeys. There had been times when chickadees would land on my hand, that was how still I could be. It's the only way to hear all of the sounds: the chipmunks prattling through the leaves, the spiders spinning.

But on this day I tumbled into a tangled land composed of twigs and glue. Somehow I felt responsible for the troubles of the night before. I was not a competent hunter, but an intruder, and my mother's disappointed face blurred my vision. Tripping and stumbling, my breath came in short gasps, loud and out of control. My arms crashed into low-hung branches and I tore through the woods like a tractor, trying to find a clearing where I could stand straight and still.

Finally, I fell flat on my face, which sank deep into the swampy forest floor. The weight of bulky clothes — the perspiration-soaked long-johns and scratchy, heavy woolens that Mother insisted I wear — sapped my strength, rendered me motionless. I felt like I had fallen into the pond with rocks in my pockets. I was dying, drowning in the aromatic pine needles, smothering in the damp moss. Then, just as I gasped my last breath of air, I felt his bear paws under my arms, lifting me high in the air like a straw doll, and I could breathe, and I could hear Father laughing, not a small laugh but the big, wide, open-mouthed roar of an unrestricted man.

FOR NOW, IT WAS OVER. THE WHOLE EPISODE had taken less than an hour and the sun had not yet risen. We gingerly picked our way out of the woods and worked our way back down the winding road to our house. I limped along slowly, as if injured.

Father spoke first, and though I could tell he was not angry, it nettled me that he had laughed so hard. My bruised pride conflicted with his lighthearted behavior and I could feel my face waving the red flag of girlish tears.

Instantly contrite, Father said kindly, "Reeni, girl, I'm sorry. I rushed you. We'll go out again and you'll see that turkey, I promise. He's glorious!"

It was a week before we went "hunting" again. Every evening after supper, when my schoolwork was done, Father sat with me at the kitchen table. In the light of the kerosene lamp, he taught me all he knew about wild turkeys while Mother rocked quietly nearby, knitting and listening.

"He's a tricky creature, cunning and smart," he said with respect. My father had the heart of an artist and as he spoke he drew a picture of a large, full-breasted turkey. The bird's sharp eyes seemed to follow me, blinking slowly and deliberately in the flicker of the light.

"He can shake your confidence, all right, and you need a bucketful of patience to find him." He stopped to think and chose his next words carefully. "And you need grace. You must walk delicately through the woods — with his kind of elegance. You can do that, Reeni. You have grace in the woods, honey." He paused and looked away, embarrassed.

Well, that certainly made me feel like a ten-dollar bill, but was I surprised, after our first hunt, to hear Father say it.

By now both Mother and I realized this turkey hunt had nothing at all to do with firearms. It had become a mission, and this time I understood that our goal was not to kill the turkey but to meet, maybe even to speak with him. One evening Father ambled into the kitchen holding a box in his hand. He said it was a turkey caller. I thought he was teasing, so I laughed.

"No, no," he said, "Looky here." He scraped a piece of slate across a hollow box with very thin wooden walls. It was about five inches long and an inch wide. The noise he made when the slate was dragged across the wood sounded, he said, like a flirting hen, calling for a tom.

"These birds are not easily fooled, you know," he told me. "The idea is to get the old boy to think we want to mate. This here device helps us to actually talk to the tom turkey, but it takes a lot of practice to make it sound like a real hen."

"The noise won't just scare him away?"

"Shouldn't. Not if we use it right and sit totally still. Also, Reeni," he said, giving me a significant look, "Don't say anything! Turkeys are afraid of unfamiliar sounds."

I took heed because, though I never did talk much, when I did have something to say, it was likely to be blurted out at exactly the wrong moment.

He practiced with the caller until it sounded like the hens I'd been hearing in the woods. With spring upon us, you could hear the wild turkeys hidden in the trees. The mating call was exotic, resonating through the woods in short staccato bursts as the birds, all anxious to mate, answered each other.

"We'll go to the same place we went last week," Father said. "A flock will travel in a circle and return to the same spot every seven days or so. I'll call for five minutes, then we have to sit quietly for ten minutes, listening. Then I'll call again." He put the caller down on the kitchen table and completed the week's lecture on the wild turkey. Mother and I sat as if in church, upright and alert.

Father stopped talking long enough to take a drink of water, and I studied his face in an effort to ascertain just exactly how important this second turkey chase was to him. I did want a close-up look of this bird that put such a sparkle in my father's eye, but my best friend Penny had invited me to spend the night at her house. She lived only two miles south on Pike Road, but had no interest in rising at dawn to trample through the woods with me and my father. Mother had already given me permission. "If you want to go," she said, "I will tell your father."

Father drained the glass of water, wiped his dripping mustache with his sleeve, and continued his enthusiastic lecture. "Come on," he said. "We've got to go outside now so I can show you how to camouflage yourself."

He hurried outside, slamming the screen door like a little boy, and any thoughts I had of postponing the turkey hunt vanished. Penny would be disappointed, but I resolved to walk down to her house with the news that, this weekend at least, I would not be spending the night with her. Molly sleepily emerged from her post under the porch and we followed my father to the big old pine tree in the front yard.

"The turkey has such good eyes that he can see us blink," Father said, and at the base of the pine he showed me how to lean against it and pull my knees all the way up to the brim of my hat. This way my face and eyes were partially covered so the turkey, if I was lucky, wouldn't notice me.

Since this was not so comfortable I asked, "Why not just hide behind the tree so he can't see you?"

"You sit with your back to the tree trunk so that you can see the gobbler before he sees you. His eyes are ten times better than yours, Reeni, and he can hear five times better! Believe me, no one can hide from a wild turkey. The best you can do is trick him."

"If another tom turkey does come in, the first boy will attack him," he continued with alacrity. "The hens will go with the winner and the loser has to find new territory." My attention must have been waning because it was unlike my father to raise his voice.

"We won't be able to speak tomorrow, Reeni. Listen to me!"

He slumped against the pine, stroking his beard the way he must have done thousands of times during his life. Molly nuzzled her needle nose deep into some nearby leaves. He waited for me to ask more questions, or at least to comment, exhibit some interest, be as excited as I was the week before.

Instead, my obstinate streak emerged, and I maintained an injured silence. Not only was my slumber party with Penny ruined, but this turkey hunt had taken on an odd and sober tone. Although Father was blind to it, Mother's resentment had not been well concealed. Her husband had never once taken her on an expedition such as this, and I felt just the slightest bit of guilt.

Father no doubt was puzzled. My lack of communication was sudden and unexplained, and we went back inside the house without another word. Like a soldier on the eve of a great land battle, I climbed the stairs to my room, resigned.

We all rose in the pearly light of dawn. The flapjacks Mother stacked on my plate held no appeal and Father ate only seven. I wore the same long johns under my heavy brown skirt and the same hard cloth coat that served every day except Sunday. I wouldn't be cold, but my high laced boots were leaky and I hoped we wouldn't walk through any streams. The air was heavy with our gravity of purpose. In some way palpable to me, a change had occurred during the seven days between the two turkey hunts. Like my father, I was not smiling when Mother held the screen door for us.

Turkeys, turkeys, turkeys, I said to myself, eyes on my father's boots in front of me. Tur-keys, tur-keys, tur-keys. I chanted the word silently, in time to our quiet march up Pike Road. Left foot, tur-key, right foot, tur-key. I began to vary the private mindsong, accenting the syllables rhythmically until soon the raucous din of my own imagination banged in my ears like many pans, one against the other.

"Remember," Father whispered, as we trudged along, "Walk two steps, listen three steps." He turned toward me and winked, and for the first time in days I relaxed.

We had been walking shoulder to elbow for a quarter of a mile up the road when Father nudged my arm and started to hoot like an owl. It was a warm deep sound, one that can make a wild turkey jealous enough to answer in his own grand gobble.

We jumped over a shallow ditch to leave the dirt road and enter the forest. The damp mid-May air tunneled deeply into my lungs, coolly caressing the dark organs of my interior. I followed Father perfectly. No twigs tangled my feet, and I ducked under the morning wet branches without a sound. Father continued hooting at irregular intervals and suddenly a short distant gobble wafted through the air.

We followed the heavily-traveled deer path to a clearing where Father pointed out the droppings and scratches on the ground. He had mentioned that acorns are turkeys' favorite food, and sure enough, I looked up to see the young leaves of an oak tree. All the signs he had painstakingly described to me were appearing as if on a map of a great treasure hunt.

Father took a seat on the ground, leaning against a softly rotting stump and motioned to me to sit across from him and to his right. I knew I should get myself comfortable because once we sat down we couldn't move again, not even to scratch our noses.

Remembering my lessons, I deliberated and chose to sit on a cushion of moss at the base of a six-bucket sugar maple. Bent into half of my height, I hoped that the turkey we heard would quickly come to our clearing in the woods.

We waited.

I hunched down in the moss and peered out of my hat into the mist. My ears hurt, I was listening so hard.

We waited.

A real owl attracted by Father's hooting landed high in the oak tree and was now noisily sending his own mysterious messages. From somewhere behind us the big bird gobbled an annoyed response to the owl. Imperceptibly, Father's hand moved to his pocket. As slowly as an earthworm, he brought out his wooden turkey caller. Three times he rapidly moved the piece of slate across the box. The sound echoed in the dense woods, eerie but effective.

Little by little, Father talked the bird closer into our sanctum. To each set of three calls — they sounded like an energetic boy running a stick across a picket fence — the turkey responded, approaching nearer, answering louder. Soon enough, I realized that they *were* talking one to another. Father was courting the wild bird in his own language. Though I was enveloped in the conversation, I couldn't gauge the turkey's location. But he was loud and he was close. Then Father said something impertinent to the tom because he left, gobbling incoherently, his voice drifting farther and farther away.

I thought it was over and started to unwind my tangled limbs but Father remained still as a stone. I froze in place, uncomfortable. In the short moment that I looked over at Father, the incredible bird decided to appear. Where he came from I do not know, but, like a phantom, the wild turkey surfaced in the center of the clearing in front of me. The blood in my veins pounded so hard and loud that I was afraid it would scare him away.

But the bird was preoccupied with the thought of a mate and paraded in a circular path with wings sweeping patterns on the muddy ground. With a flair for the dramatic, the tom stretched to his full height, perhaps three feet, and blew up his barrel chest. The long wrinkled wattle hanging at his throat was a bloody purplish-red and his satanic eyes burned a fiery amber.

I dared not look at my father. Such a vivid display unsettled me in a way that I did not understand. Though it was a brisk morning, I was sweating in my long johns.

Father explained later that the length of the black tuft of whiskers hanging from the tom's breast showed his age. This bird was in his prime; his beard showed him to be a confident three-or-four-year-old. He marched in front of us, dragging his heavy wings in circles for several minutes.

Slowly, as imperceptibly as a flower blooms, his chest expanded even fuller. He could not have grown any larger without exploding and in one undulating moment of pure passion, the wild turkey strained to display his magnificent tail feathers. Never has anyone been presented with such a fan. From deep within his throat emerged a low thunderous growl, drums rolling away in the distance. The fierce perfection made me dizzy.

My leg, hurting, involuntarily jerked hard. Pandemonium broke. As quickly as he had arrived, the turkey was gone, a running flash of huge flapping wings. I groaned in pain and sorrow, but Father, as if stung by a yellow jacket, whooped and jumped from his perch.

He danced and clapped and yahooed. He picked up a sturdy bronze feather left behind in the chaos and handed it to me with a flourish. I held it close all the way home.

Chapter Three

MY HEART WAS STILL BRISKLY BEATING AS Father and I walked back down Pike Road, passing Mother's flock of sheep. The thirty or so ewes arranged themselves in a curious row behind the insufficient fence, poking their woolly heads through the wire, lazily challenging its rusty barbs. Their interest was not in the mating dances of wild turkeys, but in the fresh, dewdropped grass just out of their reach.

That the fence needed repair was obvious — it merely suggested limits — but no matter how tempting the untrampled grass on the other side, the last thing those sheep wanted was the chaos of freedom. They shared one ram and he serviced each of them nicely. One by one, the sheep turned their rumps to us.

The closer we got to the house, the more the approaching indoors seemed foreign and irrelevant. I tried to slow the pace, finding rocks and kicking them with the intensity of an athlete in training. He didn't play the game with me, but Father was in no big hurry either.

Mother must have been standing impatiently at the parlor window, watching us saunter down the road. Usually her face was a chart of lines, an account of a farm wife's hectic work week. But there were quiet moments when she serenely gazed outside. Sweeping the lacy curtains out of the way, she would stand straight as a fresh fence post and do nothing more than watch her flock. The corners of her mouth would tremble, lifting slightly as her creased face softened. It was a face reserved for the sheep, and its unconscious suggestion of an inner life not shared with him seemed to disturb Father. Whenever he caught a glimpse of that special glow in her eyes, his own narrowed and an uncharacteristic gloominess enveloped him. His good humor blackened and vanished like cellophane in a flame.

"You watching those sheep again, Virginia?" He lobbed the words at her like bricks as we walked into the kitchen. The pleasure of the morning melted away. Their hot words filled the room like an ugly odor, trapping me at the door.

"What if I was? You and Reeni have wasted the whole morning."

"I'm getting rid of those stupid beasts," he said. His voice cracked like glass. Even the apple pie cooling on the kitchen table seemed unapproachable.

"What is the matter with you, Will Leahy?" Mother demanded. Her tone matched his. Today his cranky, unexpected monologue on the virtue of cows would not be met with moody silence. She was ready to fight.

Molly positioned herself attentively on her hairy rug behind the woodstove, ready to bolt. Father poured himself a cup of black coffee and stood at the kitchen sink. He was a man that true rancor could defeat, and his shoulders dropped as he stared glumly out the window and into the woods across Pike Road.

Mother, buoyed by the unfair attack, marched across the room to stand at the sink beside him. Unafraid, she did not even glance outside at the chartreuse canopy of early spring leaves that tinted the trees. Head cocked, facing her husband with every muscle as taut as a freshly-pulled fence, she refused to withdraw.

"What is it you're going to do? Sell my flock?" The words sizzled; she was angrier than I'd ever seen her, and the knuckles of Father's two fists were pressed hard against the kitchen counter.

Just as I opened the screen door to hide outside — the last thing either of my parents wanted was a witness — a horse snorted in the driveway. The diversion was like a magic potion. Mother and Father went quietly limp.

"Mr. Ward is here," I announced, knowing they would rather shoot each other than argue in public. They exchanged bemused looks and Father went outside to greet the insurance man, while Mother scurried to the payment envelope she kept hanging on a nail behind the kitchen door.

Mr. Ward was short and heavyset; his job obviously did not require much physical activity. He had been coming to our house once a month for as many years as I could remember. Always rumply in the same striped three-piece suit and a soup-stained tie, he was a jovial man and Mother and Father were always glad to see him. The three of them gossiped over a whole pot of coffee, long enough to divert my parents' anger.

Equally diverted, I never did tell Mother about our turkey hunt.

Chapter Four

IN REGARD TO THE SHEEP I WAS IN FULL
agreement with my mother. Father's bias was unfair, I thought. It was no secret in our house that he
would have preferred to raise larger, less resigned
cows, but he was not a dreamer. He knew that Mother
would never allow him to be a dairyman. Milking,
she believed, was for the mindless, and she was quick
to say that she'd never met a dairy farmer who didn't
smell of spoiled milk.

The topic had somehow turned into a border war
and I was not on his side. I felt no particular fondness
for the black and white heifers that dotted the landscape of our region, either. The real cows were out
west where scruffy cow punchers carried big lariats
and sidearms and seared wild-eyed cows with whitehot branding irons. Huge Longhorns with horns that
could span six feet and the bulky white-faced Here-
fords, those were cows that could be taken seriously, not like the girlish Holsteins who manufacture
distinctly feminine milk.

Like my mother, who fretted over her babies until the day she died, I continue to listen for the woeful bawl of a lost lamb. Sometimes even now, from a sleep deep in the black center of night, I know I can hear it; the sound of a frail and helpless creature awaking to the dawn of slaughter.

Just as Father taught me about turkeys, Mother taught me about sheep. "You have to plan, Reeni. Life and death don't necessarily come naturally, you know," she said, scribbling jumbled reminders onto the Turtle Brand Coal calendar that hung by the barn door. It was black with pencil marks — when to let the ewes in and out of the barn, which ones needed doctoring or special attention, when to shear.

And always, before she left the barn for the night, she bent way over the feed bunks and scratched the pink muzzles of the ewes who pushed each other out of the way, bleating for her attention. Often she returned their noisy bleats, communicating with them the way Father talked to the turkeys, and sometimes she stood still, gazing at the animals the way some people contemplate the statues of saints.

It was my mother who trained me to recognize the private nicker of a ewe gently nudging her wobbly new lamb's backside as it sucked and punched at her teats. And from my mother I learned to listen to the flock's bellwether, to act quickly when I heard the bell clanging crazily from his neck, signifying mass terror and bloodthirsty dogs. Scorched into my memory are the times Mother spotted one of those varmints or a killer coyote stalking the flock. Dropping whatever she had in her hands, she ran for the gun in the hallway and raced out the door. With the snarling face of a madwoman, she leveled and shot one, two, three times.

Mother never did have a very good aim, but a pigeon's eye was in peril when the gun was in my hands. I would kill any dog to save the lambs, but only if the poor beast was sure to drop like a pin-pricked balloon. I believe that animals should never suffer at the hands of humans, especially for following their instincts.

SNOWY WINTERS AND SLEETY SPRINGS REquired sturdy, hand-knit scarves and sweaters. Like Father, most of the dairy farmers mustered little respect for sheep, but they all kept a few. The need for warm wool to stave off the weather outweighed bias. These days you can buy soft machine-made goods at any store, but then you could say we built clothes, even food, by hand — hats and gloves, bread and butter.

Spinning wool was Mother's evening relaxation, and soft shadows danced on the walls as she coordinated her hands and feet. The repetitive hum of the wheel was as comforting as a lullaby; that the rope of spun wool from sheep born and raised on our land would be knit into a warm piece of clothing produced a rare symmetry.

Now I wear the stretchy polyester running pants that Esther picks up for me on sale at the new K-Mart in Wichner. They're comfortable — even the extra smalls are roomy — and the pretty pastel colors remind me of spring. Esther likes them because they wash up quick as a flash with no ironing. A person must change with the times, and I've always tried to be a modern thinker. But I do miss the sound of that spinning wheel and the heavy sweaters even moths could not destroy.

Mother's wheel stands motionless in the corner of the parlor now, a relic from the past. One day soon, I reckon, the farm and everything left in it will be sold to bargain-hunting strangers at McFee's Auction. I hope it doesn't rain. Nothing is more depressing than a farm auction on a wet, muddy day — unless, of course, you're the buyer. I might just pull that spinning wheel from the final auction and carry it on down with me to the grave, unless Esther wants to have it.

I'm sure she doesn't spin or even knit. She's much too busy with her family and taking care of people like me, but she always remarks on that old spinning wheel, dusts its wooden spokes. Once she even oiled the foot pedal. Esther is as stable and unpretentious as a dandelion, and she takes good care of my property, I have to admit that.

She's a Weatherby from this side of Wichner, one of those spectacled, youth-robbed women who grew up on a shoddy dairy farm. They look five years older than they are; Esther could pass for thirty-five on a good day, lately even more. They have skin the color of the milk their parents broke their backs to produce. Rising at four in the morning, the father and the mother and the children, all worked like machines, milking their cows twice a day, battling frozen water lines in the winter, pinkeye and blowfly in the summer, spending the few quiet hours fiddling with breeding statistics and puzzling over the price of corn.

Like many girls who had a taste of the dairyman's life, Esther renounced it early, moved into the heart of Wichner, and enrolled in the Carniff Community College. There she learned how to take care of invalids like me instead of the animals her parents devoted their lives to. There she met her husband-to-be, a man whose dairy farmer father had also worked himself to death. Michael Pomeroy dreamed of his own auto mechanics shop, a place with a metal sign and a New York State Inspection license. He promised Esther prosperity.

Sometimes a hint of her bygone beauty breathes a weary sigh, and for an instant a young pretty mask conceals the lines on her face. It's a narrow face which makes me think she must be hungry, but Esther is not one to eat a hearty meal. We are not at all alike: at her middle-age I was more rugged and round.

But I am still rugged enough to get out of this bed once in a while, and stubborn enough to make a last journey to the attic where undisturbed silverfish and cartons of memories await my hand. I will bide my time until Michael calls, demanding for one limp reason or another that Esther come home early. Then, I will struggle up the stairs. I will open the boxes and unfold my letters. Will they disintegrate in the light, transform from objects of soft beauty and pleasure to powder and piles of dust? I wonder about that, and how long it takes for flesh and bones to decay and disappear.

Chapter Five

Esther trimmed my nails today. It's a delicate job because they are so brittle and although she is very careful, it makes me nervous. The nails are hopelessly dry and can split like a shell, bringing tears to my eyes and pain for a week. Knowing this, Esther deliberately chose a subject she knew would distract me.

"You know, Miss Leahy," she said, "the Reverend was telling me this morning how Wichner General is the best hospital in the county."

I did not reply.

"And it's only two miles down the road from Pine Manor. I hope my mother can move there, when it's time."

She clipped my thumb painlessly short. "Where does your mother live now?" I asked, hoping to re-route the conversation.

Esther sighed. "Not too far from us. When Dad died she moved into a little apartment over in Ludlow."

"Didn't you grow up on a dairy farm, Esther?"

"Yes, indeed."

"Doesn't your mother miss it? I would feel hemmed in after living on a farm."

Esther laughed and shook the clippers in my face. "Don't you remember how hard farming was? All that haying and those machine breakdowns? We trudged through snow up to our knees twice a day just to milk some dumb cow. You must be kidding, Miss Irene. Why, Mike grew up on a farm too. He'd rather work on cars a hundred times more than work on a farm. It's just plain stupid to work that hard for nothing but the privilege of working even harder."

I didn't answer.

Esther shook her head. "I don't know about sheep, but there's nothing dumber than a cow," she muttered.

She hadn't offered her mother's feeling on the subject, but I would venture to guess that Esther doesn't know her mother as well as she thinks she does.

THE FIRST TIME I SAW EYES LIKE ESther's — dull, bewildered, and battle weary — I was seventeen years old. World War One had already taken millions of young men. Like all of the other wars in my lifetime, this one depended heavily on the patriotic fervor of rural men. My father was mortified to be rejected. He was in unshakable agreement with President Wilson's declaration of war; he even pressured me to apply to the American Women's League of Self-Defense.

"Come on, Reeni," he said. "Get with it, girl. You can shoot better than most men. Get yourself down to the town hall and teach those women how to use a rifle. It's your patriotic duty, seems to me."

In halls and churches all over America, ladies were being taught how to hold and shoot guns, attack invaders, defend the countryside; and I had every intention of protecting my homestead. Shotguns and rifles stood like polished black bones in our pine gun cabinet and my Sweet Sixteen is loaded and at the ready now, right here next to this bed, and I'll not move it, no matter what that pushy Reverend Thorne thinks.

Now that the weather has broken, the Reverend has apparently decided to visit me every week. That's what happens when your name shows up on the Social Services list. No one asks what you want, they just toss strangers at you, expecting you to gratefully swallow them whole.

The first time I laid eyes on him, shaking in his sneakers, swaying like a reed at the foot of my bed, a Mets hat churning in his hands, I knew I was in for trouble. He had barely introduced himself when he spotted the gun. "Why, Miss Leahy," he said, "you don't want to have a loaded weapon in the house, do you?"

I bristled right up. "Don't you pay it any mind,

young man. It's not very polite to walk into a person's house and criticize their belongings, you know. Not what I'd call a Christian thing to do." I thought his attire was less than godlike, too — bluejeans and some sort of fancy spring green sweater with a colorful wood duck design.

The Reverend blushed and stuttered. "No, ma'am. You're right. It's just that I see guns as an evil means to an evil end. No good can come of them, from God's point of view."

That was it. Already this scrub-faced, bible college boy was proselytizing, and we hadn't even gotten around to a civilized "good morning."

"You're not from Carniff County, are you," I said.

"No, ma'am, but I'm from Buffalo," he said, smiling hopefully, as if that made a difference. "Your case worker suggested I come out to meet you. She thought maybe we could pray together?"

Well, I told him then and there that I'd prayed only twice in my life, when my mother died and when my father died, and both times I'd forgotten the words. "I doubt you'll get this old lady into that habit," I said.

He smiled in a complacent way that made me want to curse and said he'd be back, "Just to check to see if you've changed your mind."

I CAN GUARANTEE YOU THAT REVEREND Thorne would not have felt very welcome around my father, because one thing he hated was complacency. That's why he pestered me so to join the Women's League of Self-Defense.

I was better with a gun in my hands than with a rolling pin, but I could not get my father to understand that joining a flock of women who'd never before touched a rifle was not my idea of defending the country. If that was my patriotic duty, then I preferred to spread manure.

While they giggled and flirted with the damaged boys, boys who were unfit to fight, boys whose contribution to the war effort was to teach uninterested females how to love weapons, I sat cross-legged on the grass and hoped for rain. My social skills were unusually poor, my femininity lacking in wiles, and I refused to participate. I was sure one of them would shoot me, and maybe not by accident, because my superior knowledge of guns set me apart and caused the girls to sneer.

Still, Father mistook my discomfort for complacency and insisted I join. "Show them," he urged. "Show them what you can do. Teach those girls to shoot like I taught you." But over the years Father had learned when his cause was lost on me, and finally, noting the set of my jaw, he dropped the subject. I was set free.

As the other men left town to fight on strange land, Father continued to rally his own private war effort. Every morning before dawn, he mounted his horse and traveled to farmerless farms, milking their cows, shearing their sheep, working the new soldiers' places as hard as his own.

His reputation as a master shearer followed him all over Carniff County. It took him twenty minutes to shear one ewe and at twenty cents a head he brought home a pocketful of change. But he had become one of those men who seem broken in two, unable to stand up straight, and the job caused a steady pain in his back. It was the hours bent in half between the front legs of an uncooperative sheep that kept him out of the war.

Despite his ill-tempered attitude toward the woollies, Father was proud of his reputation as a shearer. It was an important skill because the cleaner the cuts, the better quality the wool, and everybody wanted to sell their wool for the highest price. A careless shearer who cuts the greasy matts into too many small pieces ruins it; short, irregular fibers cannot be spun into a smooth and sturdy yarn.

The ballet of the shearing commenced the same way every time and the long sharp blades of the shearing tool gleamed in Father's hand. It took strength, timing and dexterity to cradle the ewe between his bowed knees. Deftly, he kicked out her back legs, simultaneously turning the mound of writhing wool upright onto her hind end. His nose could have touched the fuzzy tight stomach which bulged between the flailing front legs. Holding her steady with his left elbow, he sheared the dirty belly wool onto the ground in strips. Those thick tags of wool, heavy with mud and excrement could not be salvaged, but the long fibers which Father peeled off the ewe's body in dense layers of lanolin-soaked fleece were valuable.

Each soft clicka-click of the long-bladed scissors that cut so close to the sheep's hide is called a "blow," and Father's blows rarely opened the skin. But sometimes a large ewe, flightier than a fox-wary hen, would suddenly kick a leg free or jerk her head painfully into his thigh. One of Mother's best ewes caused the worst cut Father ever made and he was furious at the panicked sheep, and himself.

"Goddamn it!" he screamed. Loud curses like that one were startling, for Father made an obvious effort not to swear in front of children and women. The shears had carved a slice of flesh nearly three inches long on the surface of a nervous ewe's neck. Blood dripped from the large gaping cut, and her yellow eyes rolled straight up at the ceiling of the barn like a martyr preparing to die.

While he muttered through clenched teeth, I dabbed healing pine tar on the fleshy red wound to keep the flies away. He struggled with his temper. Re-positioning the half-sheared, bleeding animal between his knees, he took a deep breath and began again. The basic routine was the same every year, but every year things went differently, and every year Father could be relied upon to swear out loud, at least a little bit.

If sheep feel pain they keep their suffering a secret.

Where a goat or pig will bellow and squeal, a deep, bloody, shearing gash causes neither baa nor bleat from a woolly. I once watched a ewe struggle across two hundred yards to join the refuge of the flock. Her slack rear leg, injured in a tangle of barbed wire, dangled like a cut of raw meat. Twin lambs, unwilling to leave their mother's side, cavorted about, cheering her on while the flock far across the pasture gently bleated encouragement to her.

Like mesmerized Hindu priests, who in a frenzy of religious fervor poke spears through their cheeks drawing not a drop of blood, this ewe's singular purpose extinguished feeling. She knew that the flock could not come to her; it is the obligation of the individual to join, and the lone ewe is driven by her instinct to congregate. While the many waited patiently, baa-ing worried concern, they would not break flock rank nor imperil themselves to come to her.

But such stoicism fades at lambing. Then, lying flat on one side, her upper lip curls to show teeth and tongue while muscles strain as she pushes hard and harder, head and neck stretching upward, four hooves slipping and digging deep into the straw. It is then that the low painful bellow of delivery echoes in the still barn, and the other ewes politely wander away, allowing her the privacy that birth deserves.

As quickly as the mother ewe can manage at this primal moment, she crawls on her belly, legs splayed, to eat the afterbirth, then wills herself to her feet, for the longer the lamb goes without sucking the teat empty of its thick, waxy colostrum, the weaker it becomes. The ghostly predators — neighbor dogs, lurking coyotes, invisible bobcats — all smell the birthing. It is death if the ewe and lamb are not up and away from the telltale birth ground.

Sometimes a weak lamb simply refuses to live. They make me mad, the ones that give up so easily. The confused mother, dried placenta forlornly trailing after her in a scarlet rope, will sidle up to another ewe's newborn lamb, nudging and licking the wet little mound. She competes for its young affection, tries to steal it away, claim it for her own.

But the contented guttural language she uses to lure the lamb away is nothing more than a foreign voice, and the newborn hides behind the real mother, peeking around her full udder, afraid. The hysterical interloper cannot compete. The lamb responds only to the birth ewe whose special mothering nickers communicate to her baby; the lambless ewe folds back into the flock, sadly bleating in perplexed, prolonged tones.

The sound haunts the barn and lasts for a few melancholy hours. She must be isolated in another pen — the worst thing that can happen to a flock animal — so other lambs will not steal her extra milk. Gradually her udder deflates; the creamy flow of milk stops, the process badly tilted. Nothing can right this wrong.

Such barnyard accidents were common, not

shocking like the terrible deaths and mutilations wrought by the war. But even those ghastly horrors diminished in my mind the autumn of my seventeenth year. Reality slapped my face and everything else became inconsequential, because that was the year my father died.

Chapter Six

THE BLUE OCTOBER SKY WAS UNCOM-
monly solid. If there were any clouds, they
appeared and disappeared only when my eyes
blinked. The sun hung perfectly round and yellow as
if painted on the sapphire background by a child's
pudgy finger. The yard between the house and the
pond was covered in a colorful rug of leaves. They
tugged at my feet, begging me to kick them back up
into the air just so they could dive back down again.

But this day in 1917 was not one for play. When
President Wilson declared war on Germany early in
the spring, everyone in the county, in one way or
another, opened their veins, gushing the red blood
of patriotism. Except for my Uncle Alton who called
himself a pacifist, making my father's face go tomato
red with anger.

His army rejection was still as raw as a knife
wound, and Alton's membership in the Industrial
Workers of the World stank in Father's nose like a
week-old possum. The dangerous alliance was with

people from Wichner, and my uncle hardly knew them. Father could barely tolerate the unpatriotic action, but it kept my uncle from having to kill, which would have been, Father had to agree, an impossible act for his brother.

By fall, sheep producers all across upstate New York had been organized by the Department of Agriculture to form wool clubs. Farmers like us were eager to donate their newly sheared wool to the war effort. It took twenty fleeces to clothe one doughboy, and this breathtaking day in October our garden was harvested, our lambs were sold. Mother and I were in the back yard, washing the twenty fleeces in a tub of hot, soapy water.

There was only one blemish on this ironically peaceful day: Father's cough.

It had started suddenly in the middle of winter on an icy, diamond hard night. The exertion of spring shearing had not improved his raspy breath, nor the dry hack that crawled out of his lungs. Every time it started, in the beginning like a slow waltz then accelerating to an exhausting pitch, Mother and I were sure to avoid each other's eyes.

His bodyweight was melting away; he seemed to be disappearing. Still, he was not a smoking man, and I'd heard even worse lungs down at the general store. Molly seemed to be fading with him. Even though she ate with the gusto of a round pink-bellied puppy, she too was losing weight. Her normally shiny coat now had the luster of a sun-dried bone, and lately I'd taken to giving her extra pats, forcing her chin up into my hand and looking her straight in the eye. "Good girl," I would say, with an intensity that even a border collie could not ignore. "Good girl." And I would gently blow in her nose and scratch her ears until she yipped, escaping to return with a ball in her mouth.

The difference was she no longer pushed it to me with her nose, over and over again. Instead she looked forlorn, and collapsed with the ball between her paws, exhausted.

Mother and I had picked the chaff from the fleeces by pulling little tufts of wool apart, letting any dirt, straw, and hayseed fall onto the ground. We built a fire in the back yard, the same way we did to boil the sap to make maple syrup in March; the same way we did to boil water for canning peaches and tomatoes in August.

The hot water melted away the lanolin and grime. While Mother swished the fleece around in the tub with a wooden paddle, I wrung out small, dripping batches, placing them on a screen to dry in the sun. What had been a dirty heap of sodden fiber soon transformed into a high and fluffy pile of white wool.

We were nearly finished the day-long task and I was loading armfuls of the cleaned wool into the wagon. I had hitched Gypsy a little too soon, and being a horse with a mind of her own, she was unusually impatient and cranky. Churlishly, she tossed her head, ripping the reins out of my hands. Irritated, I raised my voice. "What is the matter with you, Gypsy? Are you in heat?"

Just then I heard Father hacking. Mother and I looked up from our work. Father and Uncle Alton had been shearing all day, and their leather boots dragged as they walked up the hill from the barn. Both men were as tired as coonhounds in the middle of the night. Molly, equally tired after a tense day of staring at the sheep, followed sluggishly at my father's heels.

"You know, that cough is getting worse, Reeni," Mother said quietly. "And he refuses to see Doc Mason."

It was the first time she had acknowledged the problem, and this was quite a bit more than an acknowledgement. Since the cough presented itself in January, I had been watching trouble grow in her eyes like cataracts in an old dog.

Shielding their eyes from the afternoon sunlight, they approached us slowly, then Father sat down on the porch steps, caught his breath and massaged Molly's bowed hind end.

"Say-hey, Ginny," he said hoarsely. "Have you seen my grinding stone? I need to sharpen these blades before I put them away for the winter." He turned the shearing scissors over and over in his cracked, thick-skinned hands. There were flecks of brown sputum on his lips.

"Whole lotta sheep were sheared with these. I bet

over two thousand, all counted." His deep breath sparked a cough that flared into a burning spasm.

When he could speak clearly he tried a weak laugh and said, "You can put this on my tombstone, Ginny. William Leahy: didn't fight for his country but sheared a lot of those stupid sheep."

"Nope," Uncle Alton said.

Father looked at him, surprised. "What do you mean, 'nope'?"

"I mean, nope, you never sheared a stupid sheep in your life. Sheep are not stupid."

Time passed as the two brothers met each other's disagreement flatly and with no familial adornments. Small, innocent discussions had lately turned sour between them; they always seemed perched on the edge of a canyon, but neither had so far jumped in.

"One of these days, we'll just have to see who can shear the most sheep," Father challenged.

"Nope," Uncle Alton said again. "You taught me everything you know about shearing, big brother. I wouldn't take that bet with your money. Just quit calling them stupid. They're not and you know it."

A straggle of light hair fell over Mother's eyes and the steamy water bathed her face in a mask of moisture. "Well, how about that, Reeni," she said. "Even your uncle can see something positive about the sheep. No wonder your father's in a bad mood today. He's feeling a little lonely in this vast sea of sheeplovers."

Father gave up, and smiled. "I'm not in a bad mood; I'm a messenger of truth, that's all."

"You've sheared more sheep than anyone in the county," I chipped in. "More than two thousand, I bet. More like . . . more like . . ." I continued, pausing for effect, trying to land on a humorous number. "I bet you've sheared twenty thousand sheep in your lifetime!"

Mother caught on and comically widened her eyes, giving an exaggerated nod. Father twisted his face in mock disbelief. "Heck, no," Alton added. "He's sheared two million if he's sheared one."

We were playacting, the tension was broken, and all of our voices joined in laughter. Then Father lost control. He doubled over, coughing like a man who would never breathe again. There was no other sound in the world. A dribble of rusty spit leaked from the corner of his mouth. It looked like the tobacco that some farmers liked to chew, but Father was not one of them.

I turned away. Uncle Alton, head buried between his shoulder blades, joined me. Even though he had sworn to do nothing for the war effort, together we loaded the wagon with armfuls of the newly-washed wool.

"COME INSIDE AND TAKE A SPOONFUL OF honey for that cough, William." Mother's words squeezed out of her thin lips in a scratchy, high catbird voice. She splashed the last mash of wet fleece into the tub of steaming water, dried her hands on her dirty apron, and practically pushed him through the screen door.

The dark, alfalfa honey, laced as it was with whiskey, did quell Father's cough. Soon his "medicine," which had been flowing rather freely, loosened his tongue, and I heard the raised but safe voices of a political discussion coming from the kitchen. They were laughing like lovers, between his loss of breaths.

It was almost dark that October day by the time I finished loading all of the wool, set Uncle Alton on the road home, and came inside to join the friendly fray, but they'd already spent their day's commentary about President Wilson and the war. Mother was stirring a black pot on the stove when Father slipped out of the back door.

"Where are you going?" Mother asked.

"Just out for some air," he replied, looking at her with a smile. He waited while Molly struggled up from her rug to go with him. "I'll take a look at that ewe. She ought to be pretty close by now."

A pregnant ewe was ready to lamb, one of Mother's favorites, and we were hoping she would throw a good-sized Christmas dinner. Mother fussed about the kitchen, flitting from the sink to the stove to the living room window, where she watched as Father headed for the barn.

Unexpectedly she said, "Keep stirring on this stew

for me, Reeni," and handed me an oversized wooden spoon. "I'm going to help your father."

Her tone was unusually gentle, her face unmarred by hard work and worry. It was as if she was slipping away to meet him for the very first time and I was embarrassed. The worry was still there, a greasy glaze in her eyes, but her voice sang, and she moved like a dancer as she gathered a mound of vegetable peels to toss to the pigs.

"It smells good," I said, positioning my red face over the kettle, inhaling the melange of vegetables and meat as if it were the tobacco I would later have the misfortune to enjoy. It would be a year before I picked up the green and red package of Uncle Alton's Lucky Strikes, a year before I would start smoking cigarettes.

We had barrels of new apples in the dark, damp root cellar, and apple pie always caused my father to whoop it up and slap his knee hard. "You can start a pie for your father, too, Reeni. That will improve his spirits." It was the last time her tone was natural and full; thereafter, if I think back correctly, she herself became reedy and weak. She took an unusually long and sweeping look around the kitchen, as if drinking in the final moments of life as she had known it.

I lit a kerosene lamp and quietly slipped through the cellar door. Rodents — small mice and the occasional gigantic rat — were likely to be making munching noises and I listened carefully before I walked down the cellar steps. I knew the root cellar well, knew that the potatoes were in baskets at the bottom of the stairs to my left and that the apple barrels and beets were on my right. Straight ahead were shelves of jars filled with tomatoes and jams and peaches and beans. It was food that sustained us through times when dollar bills were as scarce as bald eagles.

I filled my apron pockets with the apples, so aromatic that they overwhelmed the heavy muskiness of the cellar, and hurried back upstairs, surprised that my parents had not yet returned.

I thought it was the new lamb — maybe twins or triplets — that caused the delay. The lamb could present totally backwards and need to be pulled instantly, otherwise it could inhale and drown in the uterine fluid. Perhaps it had one or both legs bent in the birth canal. Someone has to insert a finger or hand and pull hard to straighten the lamb's leg. Or twin lambs could be entwined like a pair of prayerful hands, a dangerous, complicated tangle that would require the skillful penetration of the shepherd's arm. I added water to the stew, stirred to keep it from sticking, added just enough hardwood to the stove, started to make the biscuits Father liked to have with his supper.

As I kneaded the biscuits I imagined the two of them in the barn, bending at the waist to get a better view of the ewe — the parts so much like a woman's that you'd be embarrassed to look if you weren't a vet or a farmer — checking to see that the birth was normal.

Sometimes, before the ewe grunts down on her side in the one place she has pre-selected to lamb by pawing and pacing and pawing, you can see the small pink moon nose of the lamb resting on two front feet. The uterine membrane has not yet broken and through the viscous, wetly round, pale amber balloon filled with unborn lamb, you can see its closed eyes, its mouth contentedly moving, ready to suck. There is no need to interfere. The mother ewe eventually lies down, the sack lets loose with a wash of fluid and the undulating process of birth begins.

I myself never had a child, nor a marriage, and never felt the need for either. But I have delivered a few babies, and the way a woman delivers at home in the bed can be awfully close to the way a ewe delivers in the barn. It's a resemblance that makes me smile — a hundred-and-fifty-pound woman who will have a five or ten pound infant isn't a far cry from a pregnant ewe. Preachers think they know all there is to know about birth and death, Reverend Thorne being no exception, but it's the farmers and veterinarians who can tell you the truth.

Biscuits ready, I added yet more water to the stew, still confident my parents needed no help, and began to peel the apples. Mother was expert and Father, lukewarm about sheep or not, would rather die than cause any animal unnecessary pain. More likely, I thought, the two of them were tarrying in the barn on this warm autumn evening, inhaling the warm, moist, scent of unspoiled being.

I WAS WRONG.

Flies stood boldly on his lips by the time I saw my dead father and I did not see the moon-eyed madness that slashed my mother's purple face until I finally went to the barn myself. Molly cowered, whimpering like a starved dog in the darkest corner while new healthy twin lambs cavorted in the hay, nuzzling their exhausted mother.

Like a self-flagellating penitent, my mother crept to me on hands and knees. Bleeding and covered in hay and manure, she moaned in a desolate agony that my father, at least, did not have to hear.

One thing the sheep did, they evened the score with him. Mentally as well as physically, for in the odd way that some men react to such things, my father was a bitter man when it came to fighting for his country. Because of the sheep, his honor had been snatched away.

A few days after Father was buried up on the hill, when Molly could no longer stand to wait for him to come in the back door, I found her dead on her rug in the kitchen. I dug a grave for her with my shovel and buried her under the apple trees near Father and my mysterious brother Billy. I laid her braid rug on the floor of the dark hole and wrapped her in one of Father's flannel shirts.

It is callous earth that covers an unshrouded beast, and when Joe, who is tired now as am I, noses my covers for the last time, I will see that he, too, receives a proper rug to lie on and a pillow for his head. But now he is snoring at the foot of this bed and my eyes are heavy with sleep.

Chapter Seven

REVEREND THORNE DOES NOT UNDER-
stand that not everybody in this world turns to his
brand of religion for their comfort. Earlier today he
politely refused Esther's offer of a cup of tea. "No,
thank you very much," he said, winking at her. Then,
as if I had invited him to do it, he dragged a chair
from the kitchen and sat right down next to my bed.

"But I do want a word with my favorite lady,"
he says. "God certainly is smiling on Wichner today,
Miss Irene. Forsythia is in bloom in everyone's yard.
It's not a bad little town, with those huge Victorian
houses, and when the crabapples bloom on Main
Street, the place will be just magnificent."

He leaned in closer to me, as if I wasn't getting his
point. "You know, Wichner does have a moviehouse,
and a really talented theater group, and no one can
complain about the library."

"I know what Wichner has," I replied, eyeing his
new leather boots. "You think I'm such a hillbilly I've
never been to town?"

Well, the poor man crumbled like a sundried petal, and Esther banged a pot and gave me a dirty look from the kitchen stove. I did feel a little sorry for him. Still, I reason, if some self-proclaimed messenger of God is going to try to change my life *and* wear cowboy boots, then he should be prepared for a bit of resistance.

More kindly, I said, "I do not want to move twenty miles from this farm. To me, that would be like moving to Hawaii."

"Then how about we pray together. There's a first time for everything."

"Dear God," I said, brightly. "Please remove this man from my presence."

Luckily, the preacher does have a little sense of humor. He shook his head and laughed. "What a handful you are, Miss Irene Constantine Leahy. What a handful."

SOME PEOPLE, MY FATHER WAS ONE OF them, turn to the sky or the sea or the dirt underfoot for consolation and calm. I concentrated on the lonely sound of the wagon wheels, churning through the dark, dead leaves that covered Pike Road, and the sweet, musty smell of my horse. Mother had sent me to the Daltons with father's measurements. Mr. Dalton needed them to build the coffin, a job he did on request, for no money. I guess you could call it a hobby.

One of the many rules that attended death demanded that the body be washed and dressed before it stiffened; otherwise, it couldn't properly be laid out in the parlor. I waited at the Dalton place with the cotton-headed sense that at that moment the single most private act between two people was occurring between my parents.

It had been midnight by the time Mother and I lifted Father's unwieldy body into a wheelbarrow, pushed him up the bumpy hill from the barn to the house, and arranged him on the davenport. He couldn't have looked more unnatural. Alive he would have caught hell if Mother had seen him lying there in his workclothes. Such a luxury was reserved for the dead.

"What about Uncle Alton?" I whispered hoarsely to Mother. We were both exhausted and the long night had just begun.

She stared blankly at my face, and I repeated my question.

"Shouldn't I go get Uncle Alton?"

"By now your uncle is dead drunk, Reeni. I'll tell him tomorrow." She spoke each word as if it would not take meaning unless I heard every vowel and consonant separately.

I had seen my uncle drink before, but I'd never heard the work drunk applied to him. Mother's assertion seemed overwrought and mean. I was glad to get away.

So while I sat at the Dalton's kitchen table, Mrs.

Dalton saddled her pretty chestnut mare and went to be with my mother. It took the rest of the night for Mr. Dalton to build the pine box, to pad it with horse hay, lining that with a soft, creamy white material. Left alone in the unfamiliar kitchen, I cradled my head on the table and escaped into sleep. I was startled as a bird to feel Mr. Dalton's hand rub soft, wide, wakening circles on my back. Those few empty moments before I was fully awake were precious and fleeting.

Through the cheerful kitchen curtains I could see the early morning sun decisively claiming the land, brushing the fields with a cold October light. "Can you help me with it, Reeni?" Mr. Dalton asked gently, and I nodded.

As we loaded the sturdy pine box onto the wagon, I heard in the distance the lonely chime of the church bell. It tolled forty-two times, one for each of Father's years on earth. Mr. Dalton and I, motionless, listened to the sound travel through the hills. I wondered how my Uncle Alton was taking the news, how adrift he would be set.

The last bell sank into silence and Mr. Dalton asked, "Do you want me to take you home, Reeni?"

"No, thank you, sir," I replied, squeezing his muscular upper arms with the gratitude of an adopted pet. Both of us understood that just as building the coffin was his tribute to my father, taking the long wooden box home would be mine.

That day people streamed to our house, for my father was a well-liked man. Fewer will mourn my passing. It's a side effect of longevity, as I've attended more funerals than I can remember. Just this afternoon Esther read me two familiar names in the obituary page. Every week there is someone I know, but I no longer go to their funerals. Why should anyone come to mine?

But that day is a clear and unforgettable memory. Farmers and their wives arrived in wagons and on horseback, laden with baskets of food and sympathy. Nearly everybody from our town and many from surrounding hamlets came to pay their respects. The women, all in bonnets and dark long dresses, hovered in the kitchen. Rearranging the refreshments, sometimes forgetting to hush their tones, they spoke of my father and the war, and the promised land.

"The nicest man, he was," Cecilia Roberts was saying. "I still owe him for last year's shear."

"Well, pay up now, Cece," Mrs. McWilliams snapped. "They'll need every penny. I'm a widow. I know how hard it will be."

My mother's face was round and red from crying, and the braid usually so tightly wound on top of her head was crookedly loose. She refused to move from Father's desk, testing the neighbor women's abilities to divert her, oblivious to all of their attempts.

As each failed: "Come, Virginia, you must eat something," I watched my mother swell like a blowfish, ready to burst with the shock of her loss. I myself sat in a taciturn lump on a bench in the kitchen, waiting for the misery to end. How could it be that Mother was more stricken than I? Did her bloated face, and the round blotches of tears that darkened her blouse prove that she cared more? And why could I not squeeze even one tear from the marble eyes burning in my head like hot desert sand?

The men gathered outside. With faces covered in not necessarily clean beards, they meandered in small groups, talking quietly on the porch, shaking their heads. I heard Mr. Ward trying to sell Gabriel Lacruce a life insurance policy. "Best thing you could do for your family," he said. "Will Leahy knew what he was doing, all right. Took good care of his womenfolk."

Even now, remembering that time, I gasp for air like a hooked carp: the waving motion of those people in our house, their faces drifting back and forth over my face, into my eyes, and my mouth and nose like water lapping a wrecked ship on the beach. They took my breath away.

The ladies directed the burial day with hands of experience. The coffin, balanced on two skirted sawhorses, had been set between the front windows where closed curtains set a kind of a stage. When it was time, after everyone filed through the parlor, and stepped up to take one last look at their friend and neighbor, Mary Cunningham somberly nodded to the four self-conscious men waiting for her signal. Looking like sheepish little boys, they hoisted the pine coffin out of the house and onto the wagon.

The house slowly emptied.

Chapter Eight

THE TEMPERATURE THIS MONTH OF MAY has traveled the road from hot to cold and back again in a most distressing way. My bones cannot adjust fast enough to these extremes. Esther is constantly tucking in my blue-veined feet, feet that seem supernaturally attached to this remnant of a body, feet whose bunioned toes cannot tolerate even the suggestion of a sock.

But anyone who lives in this part of the country knows that the weather here is capricious. The day of Father's funeral had been just like this one, turning from a steamy afternoon to a raw and chilly one. As Mother and I stepped into the wagon to ride up the hill to the Leahy plot, a cold breeze blew up, grabbing at our hats and hair.

Windy squalls sent weed kitties tumbling across the field. As we neared the top of the hill, we could see Reverend Moore leading hymns. Father was going to be planted like a potato in the rocky land we called ours, and no number of hymns led by Reverend Moore's kind would change that truth.

Uncle Alton, pale and hungover, had insisted on driving the wagon, but even I could tell he was as wobbly as a one-legged rooster. Gypsy knew when he touched the whip to her rump that something was wrong. She galloped up the hill, ripping through the dry autumn underbrush like a horse possessed, heading straight for Reverend Moore. Suddenly she whinnied and reared as if she'd seen flames.

The wagon raised perpendicularly to the ground, and the pine box slid out, tilted, and coasted down the hill like a waxed sled. Everyone else stood on the top of the hill; there was no one to divert the runaway coffin.

Uncle Alton desperately tried to control the horse, while I wrapped my arms around my mother's rounded shoulders. Whispering nonsense in her ear, I watched in horror as my father's coffin gathered momentum, bounced and rolled, scraped and skimmed the colorless grass all the way to the bottom of the steep slope. Finally it lodged in a splintered heap against the best apple tree on the farm.

The story of Father's funeral grew to gruesome proportions. People said otherwise, but the coffin had been securely nailed and though it was split, it did not break open. Contrary to rumors that still exist today, we did not call the service off altogether. A few men hoisted the rebellious coffin onto their shoulders. Mother and I, dazed, disheveled, and dirty, followed, while Gypsy, successfully free-ing herself from the wagon, ran haywire somewhere down in the valley.

When we reached the grave, Mother took both of my hands and looked me in the eye. The rough wind gusted again, played with our skirts. Apples thud-ded to the ground all around us, and suddenly my mother smiled. The strain of the day had stripped us both, and giggles erupted slowly until we were roar-ing with laughter, until tears flowed like rivers down our cheeks.

Father would have approved.

And so we laid him down to a windy rest right next to Billy. It's where my father expected to land, but not for at least another thirty or forty years. Now that innocent plot holds everyone in my family ex-cept me, and I'm closer than ever to bunking in the muddy brown earth.

Why one yearns for a certain piece of ground in which to sleep for eternity is a question I cannot an-swer. But I feel I must be buried on the hill next to my mother and father, next to my brother Billy, near poor Uncle Alton whose life was either interesting or mishandled, depending on your point of view, near Molly and the other loyal sheepdogs. I will never rest otherwise. All of my life that fraternity of the dead, who lived underground on the hill overlooking the apple orchard, was on my side. It is suitable that I join them; together we should return to the soil.

But it's against the law these days to bury the dead

in their own backyard, on their own property. Someone will try to bury me in strange dirt away from my family, I just know it. It will be a low thief who steals my ghostly view of the house where each of our lives proceeded upon their rugged trails. I suppose a tenacious fear of straying from this farm is what keeps me alive. Already I've outlived simplicity.

The customs of this modern world often exclude the obvious; the beauty of tending the grass that will grow on your own grave is deemed eccentric, even morbid and irreligious.

A woman has few surprises when her days are numbered; I can't speak for the men. They seem to be astonished by the passage of their years; that their muscles falter under the weight of a hay bale, that their hair thins and their hands crack. Their brains go from hard to soft-boiled, and they're always astounded. And though a farmer may be more proud of his barn than his house, he is often more vain, too. He worries about looks, his own or his wife's, his horse or his cows. That, I suppose, is one reason there's so many widows living out here in the hills.

Chapter Nine

IT WAS DEEP IN THE BLUE WINTER, MANY weeks after Father's death, and snow hung like pajamas on the limbs of the apple trees. Mother and I were in process, still adjusting slowly to our new situation. She had not returned to any of her regular daily chores, and after a frigid day of working with Uncle Alton in the barn, I was particularly tired. Yet I was the one doing the dishes while she sat reading in the rocker in front of the fireplace. I stared out of the window above the sink, watching the cold, bony apple trees gyrate in the wind.

Of all the trees stripped naked by the winter's rush, the apples seemed to me the most exposed. Their frail nudity aroused an odd maternal instinct, and I wished for a blanket as big as the sky, thick enough to spread over and protect them all.

Sometimes Esther stands at the kitchen window exactly as I did, watching those same twenty-two apple trees that still sway like sailors at the base of the cemetery. I wonder what she is thinking, if she tires of doing chores for me, the way I grew tired of doing them for my mother. That day, so long ago, an inexplicable rage at my mother rose like a welt. I wiped my hands on a tea towel and turned to face her.

She was thumbing through the gold-edged pages of the Leahy family Bible that Uncle Alton had retrieved from some dark corner of my father's life. He had offered it to her humbly, with two hands, and only a little liquor on his breath. While I understood that it was his peace offering to her, I did not believe that my father ever opened a Bible. But she accepted the book as if it, like her brother-in-law, was a heavy burden.

Maybe it was the presence of the massive Bible, or Mother's unkind treatment of my uncle. Maybe it was the icy, vulnerable trees childishly stretching to the sky, or maybe I was just bone-tired, but when I turned from the sink I was in the mood for a battle. Flippantly I said, "So what does that Bible say, Mother, did the apple shut us out, or lead us into the Garden of Eden?"

I spit the words out of my mouth like watermelon seeds. My argumentative tone was enough to cause a reaction of fury, since Mother allowed for no humor in matters of religion.

She stared at the page in front of her. I watched a red flush travel into the roots of her hair which had so thinned that I had lately begun to check my own brush. Why couldn't I control myself? I wished so hard I'd kept quiet that it must have shown.

But in the space of a turn of the Bible's page

she smiled, and after another page she laughed out loud. Soon her mouth was wide open and I could see the terrible black holes where teeth were once rooted. The only other time I'd seen her laugh this way had been on Father's burial day, but this time it frightened me for I was not laughing. Her eyeballs quivered in their sunken sockets, and I stepped back.

"You'll have to ask someone else that question, Reeni," she finally sputtered. "I guess there's never been another fruit quite so biblically burdened." She sank her face into her apron and furiously wiped her eyes. Still chuckling, she returned to the cryptic pages. I was dismissed.

She was right about apples, though. Not only do poor Adam and Eve bear the blame for every ill known to mankind, but the legends and myths surrounding the fruit that so tempted them are endless. Is it true that a woman should roll under an apple tree to induce pregnancy? Or that washing your face with the apple tree sap unleashes its powers of love and fertilization? Does an apple a day keep the doctor away, and did Indians really use slices of the fruit to clean their teeth?

Reverend Thorne likes to say, "The Master has a plan," but if that's so, why not give me the answers now, when they would be useful? Soon enough I will join those who did not outlive the apple trees, and I will be the most furious dead person in the ground if, as I suspect, there are no answers to my questions.

Chapter Ten

Farm life assures an intimacy with both gains and losses. Esther took me to Dr. Coughlin for my annual checkup in Wichner last week and we saw a lamb, throat cut, hanging from a tree limb in a front yard. Blood pooled on the grassy ground inches from her nose.

Esther groaned. "I'm sorry you had to see that, Miss Irene," she said. "It's the Marzullo dairy. They raise a lamb or two every year."

I craned my neck as she sped past.

"Well, that lamb will make some fine chops," I said. "I read that people are beginning to raise their own food again. Too many contaminants in store-bought produce. It takes more than throwing some corn into a feeder, I'll tell you that much. You have to respect the animal, give it the best life possible. Then you earn the responsibility of killing it well. All it really takes is a balanced mind."

Esther, her chin trembling, said nothing and I was

sorry, for I should have kept these musings to myself. I had spoken like a sharp-tongued old woman, without thinking about her feelings. If I keep doing that, Esther's loyalty will erode and I will deserve to be left alone.

In the beginning, the loss of my father was more than a matter of his empty space, although that, eventually, caused me to retch with grief in the dead of the night. Countless black hours within icy bright days passed in a swirling pattern of sleep. But finally youth and the first modest scent of acceptance teased me out of the darkness.

The flexibility of my eighteen years mounted a shaky defense, and when the apples blossomed in the spring of 1918, I transplanted some wild tiger lilies to his grave. By mid-summer, when their victorious heads shot straight up like trumpets, my grief was nudged into a dusty little box that I opened and closed at will. Like the original apple trees, some of the flowers divided and multiplied into unkempt thickets along Pike Road. I can look out of the window from this old brass bed where I spend most of my hours now and see them still — all stamen and pistil and turbulent orange.

It was an undebatable fact that my father no longer existed in this world, but his specter continued to occupy every facet of the farm. His image lived just outside of my vision's reach. Like the ghostly feral cats who annually invade the barn, no matter how fast I turned my head, they stay beyond my sight, evaporating like mist every time I tried to catch a glimpse.

My mother never outgrew the loss. It's not so hard to explain, now that I understand. When people live together day in and out, every minute in some way underlined by each other's actions, it becomes easy to love and hate simultaneously. Her pain sank deep into her soul, grasped her heart and drained her vitality. But even she, in time, healed just a bit and was not entirely ruined.

The inappropriate bursts of open-mouthed laughter, an unsettling habit that began the day we buried Father, slowly vanished. Her distressed compulsion to read the Leahy family Bible faded.

On her fortieth birthday, a year after she found Father dead in the barn, my mother came down the stairs from her room in a fancy dress. "I was married in this dress, Reeni," she told me. "Don't you worry about me from now on, dear. Just let me have this day in peace." She patted my arm, adjusted my braids. "It can be my birthday present."

From early morning until the sun set, she sat motionless on the grass of Father's grave. I peeked through the kitchen curtains and watched her, myself motionless, until finally she kissed his and Billy's gravestones, returned to the house, and without a word went to bed.

The next morning she watered the houseplants and pruned the wily philodendron. She began to care again for her sheep and lambs, and began once again to garden, but a part of her had withered like a leaf and fallen away.

As my mother dried into crisp stems and seeds, I blossomed. Her juices seeped into me, and while it was hard to live without my father's wide smile and steady approval, I began to enjoy groping in the darkness of the future.

MOTHER WAS IN A NERVOUS MOOD THE DAY I claimed Father's desk. It was scarred even then, an old pine table that sat in a corner of the kitchen, out of the way and next to the pantry. We had been fluttering around it like gossamer-winged bugs, neither of us willing to assume his space. But the collection of overdue notices and unanswered letters, the paperwork that my mother would not, or could not address, needed attention. The more I nagged, the less attention she paid to the growing pile.

Boldly I pulled out my father's sturdy T-back chair, and sat down at his desk. With that swift motion, as sure as the swoop of a hungry hawk, I became the head of the household while Mother, silently relieved, patted my shoulder and put on a pot of fresh coffee.

For the first few days I did not touch a thing. I sat upright and girlish, brushing out my braids, staring at the pieces of paper, important wisps of information that shape daily life. But bit by bit, I addressed our finances. I opened Father's magazines and studied the newest techniques in ovine medicine. I moved some of Father's things, rearranged his books, and added some of my own. My unbraided hair was long and annoying, falling in my eyes as I hunched over my work.

One late night, after Mother had gone to bed, I opened a desk drawer and found a small black notebook lying under a pair of sheep shears. Penciled in a cursive that combined his delicate artistry with his strong self-confidence, were Father's last notes. "Shear Burdick's sheep Tuesday" and "Ask Aubrey about seed spuds" and "Mend Tillie's fence."

I stoked the fire. One by one, in a ritual of finality, and barely able to see, I burned each piece of paper. The papers themselves meant little to me: it was his handwriting that salted my eyes and steamed my glasses.

Dazed, I went to the mirror that hung on the parlor wall. I turned the oil lamp to its highest flame and set it safely on a table. The shears were still sharp as a razor and quickly, before I could think, I lopped off my hair, first one side, then the other, then, I pruned my whole head and threw the light brown pile into the fire. A brief but pungent smell filled the room.

Mother claimed my hair made me look like a man, but it was, in fact, the only haircut to have if I didn't want farmwork and machinery to twist my head off like a bottlecap. Each morning before I fed the animals, with a cigarette and a cup of strong black coffee at hand, I reviewed my work list, paid bills, tended to paperwork. I oversaw the homestead with the fervor of a factory foreman whose job is on the line.

In the clutter of books and papers, bank statements and bills, I found on Father's desk another thick book full of handwritten notes. The pages were covered with notations on the trees in our orchard. With colored pencils he had sketched each variety, showing their shapes — conical, round, oval, flat — features of the skin — blotchy, freckled, blemished or not. On the back of his sketch, arranged in careful columns were all the characteristics of the specific breed. Texture, Shape, Size, Color of Skin, Flavor, Storage Life, Remarks.

The stems on each apple were penciled in brown — short and stubby, or long and thin. Rusty or fiery red, banana yellow or green, his sketches were true to the variety of the fruit he grew. In the notebook were also musings that bound me tight to the desk where he wrote them:

"Soft apples, like soft people, bruise easily. Then, the first sign of damage allows the sad brown color of decay to take over the fruit. Soon insects swarm the apple, eating and sucking the dying pulp. Yellow jackets delve deep into the finished fruit, a danger to those many dogs who like to nudge and chew the fallen apple. But horses are known to take their chances, too, eating fruit that has dropped to the ground and fermented. Probably the first hard cider was

made by some observant medieval person who noticed his steed circle, then fall in a drunken heap under an apple tree. The rotting flesh of mammals gives no gift — no hint of cider nor even a useful vinegar — but foul fruits and vegetables can offer gallons of cheer."

The fruit of the apple tree is the fruit of my land. Apple jelly, pies and crisps, apple butter, and cider and jack, vinegar and wine and a walk through the field with an apple to chew. These things were all provided by the apple trees, which struggled against the devious maggots and spores. Let the skin blemish and the apple will soon be soft brown rot. Let the first sign of scab — a descriptive enough disease — appear, and the fruit will shrivel helplessly.

Even a branch knocked dead by a stormy wind can provide a final pleasure. Apple wood burning a golden flame in the fireplace on the night of a harvest moon is not a perfume that can be bottled.

This is the sadness of my age: I will never bite into the crisp hard flesh of a Baldwin again, nor hear the satisfying sound of its tough skin cracking open. Never again will I sink my teeth deep into its core, half of the thing filling my mouth, freezing the inside of my cheeks as the watery sweetness of it drips coldly down my chin.

Tonight I will ask Esther to dish out a bowl of applesauce. In this way, perhaps, I can suck on the taste of my youth. The beauty of an apple is how many dresses she can wear. The applesauce Esther cans and brings to line my shelves like jars of cinnamon soldiers and the sinfully smooth apple butter are the only ways I can enjoy an apple these days.

What a terrible loss.

Chapter Eleven

———————

The NIGHT WAS STILL, THE GROUND covered in feet of snow. Three years had passed since first I'd assumed possession of my father's desk. The bills were always paid in a timely fashion; the barn was full of well-fed lambs. Slowly my mother and I had developed a life alone, together.

Warm fireshadows from the wood Uncle Alton brought in performed like graceful dancers on the parlor walls. Mother set aside her knitting and shakily lifted a cup of hot apple cider to her lips. Her arthritic knuckles had become as round as marbles, but she was always able to knit.

Though the January 1921 issue of *Rural New Yorker* was open on my lap, I had been lulled away from my reading material, "The Modern Shepherd." This icy night my gaze was drawn to the fire, my concentration melted by the flames.

Our farmhouse, like so many others, revolved around the fireplace, a testimony to the practicality of the nineteenth-century builder. On the first floor were three shallow hearths, one each in the parlor, the kitchen, and the small handyman's room where my mother had finally agreed to allow Uncle Alton to live, as long as, she said, he brought no liquor into her house.

Upstairs, the chimney was hidden under wallpapered lathe and plaster. If the house burned to the ground, a mass of hand-laid fieldstone, thirty feet high from the dirt floor cellar to the top of the chimney, would stand like an Egyptian obelisk.

Heavy-lidded, I was half asleep in the honey glow of the burning applewood when I heard Mother's sharp cry of pain. She had prodded the fire, and like an ornery cat, it spit. A cherry blush spread like a stain across her cheek. I applied gobs of hog lard to the hot skin, but a blister was assured. By the time the pain and panic were tended, it was well past our early bedtime. Mother had already started up the stairs when she said, "What was that?" At first I thought the brief beam of light was a reflection, and I said so.

"No," Mother said, "It's something outside. Look, there it is again." At the second flash, she came back down the stairs and pulled aside the kitchen curtain. We stood next to each other, peering out of the window, straining our eyes.

"Maybe someone was walking down the road with a light," I said. It would have been unusual, but the odd light *could* have been the flicker of an oil lamp.

Mother thought it looked like a bolt of lightning,

but that was impossible; the stars were bright as crystal plates in the black sky and the snow was a quiet blue in the moonlit darkness.

"What do you think it was, Irene?" Mother asked timidly. She was upset about the burn, fretting about the fire, weary with the bottomless patience unique to old women and dogs. "Do you see anything?"

"Not now. Maybe it was a shooting star," I said. Her hands were cold, trembling like two frightened sparrows. I rubbed them with my masculine, farm-callused palms.

We gazed out of the window at the tree limbs that cracked in the cold, motionless and blue and oddly comforting. Mother leaned against me, her skin pale and flawless around the ugly discoloration dominating her cheek. Neither of us spoke as we watched the long, still shadows of the trees reclining on the snow.

Finally Mother whispered, "It doesn't hurt at all now, Reeni. Do you think it will scar? You know I've been so lucky about that. Even you have a scar on your face, don't you, Reeni?"

I had been twelve, picking Northern spy apples in the orchard, when I tumbled off the ladder. Most of the branches whipped harmlessly around my head, but one fingerthick limb slashed my forehead. The jagged furrow was unsightly and permanent. Thereafter I pulled my pale hair forward, allowing it to escape in straight, concealing bangs over my eyes.

The talk about my down-to-earth scar dashed any grandiose thoughts about the universe I might have entertained. "Let's go to bed, Mother," I said. "If we dress that blister again in the morning, you won't get a scar." I told her this, but in truth I expected a mark — it was a deep burn, the kind that could kill the cells of the skin.

I opened the back door and called the dog — Jacky it was at that time. In the full face of the luminous night, I could see her canine footprints headed toward the barn. The trapezoidal pattern was single-minded; I had waited too long and Jacky had decided to spend the night with her sheep. Another one of our complicated border collies, I was never sure that Jacky trusted me, although she wagged her tail like a puppy when Mother came into the room. I called her one more time, then shut the door. It was warm enough in the barn for a dog.

The night seemed exceedingly quiet. I took an apple from the fruit bowl and crunched into it, breaking the silence, startling myself. I noted that Uncle Alton had not yet come in for the night. "I'm going over to Annie Somers tonight," he had told me earlier, winking broadly and patting the flask in his back pocket. Apparently, fat old Annie Somers had a crush on him.

Once undressed and snuggled under the covers, I could not sleep. Restlessly, I re-lit the oil lamp and picked up a magazine; twenty minutes passed before I drowsily blew out the flame. My eyes had not quite adjusted to the darkness when suddenly I saw the flash again. The strange light traveled back up the road. This time, though, it didn't flicker. It stayed bright and steady, and as it moved closer to the house I listened hard, and then I remembered.

I was willing this once to forfeit the night's silence; I wanted to hear the mutter of the motor on my own Pike Road, a dirt road so narrow that four decent pulling ponies could not have passed. Slowly the round headlights emerged, casting complicated shadows in the trees, slicing through the woods with the sharpness of a fishwife's knife. I threw open my bedroom window.

The automobile passed the house in a flurry of snow, a great black bear sliding down the hill. I realized then that as quickly and unkindly as the fire had seared my mother's face, an era had vanished. Even here, in these suspicious hills; even here, where money is scarce and people cling to common sense; even here, in my own time, the horse would die, the wagon would rot away.

Chapter Twelve

THE VERY FIRST ANIMAL I SAW DIE UNDER the wheels of a car was a squirrel.

I'd always thought of squirrels as nervous little creatures, but this one was as casual as a fuzzy gray bedroom slipper. He strolled down the middle of the road, dropped a nut, and swished his tail, picked up the nut and swished his tail, dropped it again and picked it up, until abruptly, he sat still on his haunches, listening. Tail curled gracefully high, he tilted his head. The car, black as a crow and just as noisy, was only feet away when the animal, confused by the rumbling ground and the size of the approaching monster, darted right under its wheels.

That day I asked Uncle Alton to build us a fence in front of the house and the dogs, with their exceptional border collie intelligence, got the connection and never strayed into the road. I've lost a few cats, though, over the years. Felines are adverse to restriction and some bird hunters will run over them on sight because they raid nests and eat wild chicks.

As Esther says, natural balance is not necessarily agreeable to humans.

Roadkill is a common sight these days — bloodied dogs and rabbits, cats and chipmunks, raccoons and possum and turtles crushed by a changing world. Cars kick up dust on Pike Road like horses at a rodeo. They spew grime on my windows and the clothes Esther hangs outside to dry. I know what's coming because I read it in *Time* magazine. Reverend Thorne brings me his copy every week and I read it religiously.

Soon enough, my dirt road will be laid thick with asphalt, turned into a highway or a thruway or a beltway, a freeway or a turnpike, an artery or circle. There will be bumper-to-bumper cars, horns blasting, radios panting, that's what's coming to my Pike Road. Maybe not now, but one day.

"THERE GOES YOUR FAVORITE NEIGHBOR," Esther said, glancing out of the window. She giggled as a pickup truck thundered by the house, rattling over the deep potholes.

Well, as Esther knows, where Jim Sinclair is concerned, I am never without opinions. "He drives too fast," I say, annoyed. "He'll break an axle if he's not careful."

There are people — Sinclair is one of them — who are bound to annoy a person like me. They make more noise than the average person is allotted; they don't understand the place they've chosen to live. They don't savor the winter like those of us who were born to it and complain bitterly when the summer is cooler than expected, the shadflies more numerous, or the deer too elusive. They speed down a dirt road in a sparkly new pickup like a bat out of hell, forgetting that the ground heaves in the spring and they could lose control.

I myself would not trade money for those January days when I was still active, when the temperature was below zero and the sun was so bright and orange that it felt like hot quarters on my eyes. The red barn boards creaked with the cold, and snow slid from the roof, startling the animals as they snorted and joggled in the hay. The water I carried from the house froze in the pail, its thin skin of ice forming delicately, floating on the top like crumpled cellophane.

FROM MY BED I CAN SEE STRAIGHT INTO THE kitchen. A can of Campbell's soup is sitting on the counter. Is it tomato or chicken noodle? That I cannot tell. But as the morning air pours like light through the cracks in the windows, either will do. Perhaps by Memorial Day the weather will be less jittery.

I did not hear Esther come this morning; I seem to be sleeping longer and more deeply than normal. I did not hear Reverend Thorne knock at the door either, but there is his jacket, hanging on a kitchen chair. There's an odd feel to the house, as if it's filled with invisible people. Even Joe is not on his bed at the foot of mine.

I don't worry that the Reverend will poke into my journal; his nature would not allow a sneaky invasion. Esther, though, might be tempted. After all, the notebooks are strewn wide open on my bed, and I would read hers, if she had one, if I had the chance. The better I get to know Esther, the less I seem to know about her.

I do know she lives on the Star Route four miles south of the city of Wichner in a new green and white trailer. Well, it's what I call a trailer, but she is quite frosty on that topic.

"It's a double-wide, Miss Irene. A double-wide," she said, when I asked where she'd set up her "trailer". The nasty look you sometimes see in a ranging rooster settled in her eye.

"Now don't be touchy," I said. "People have to live somewhere, but I hope you don't expect houses made out of tin to last a hundred and fifty years. I don't mean to offend you Esther, but get that husband of yours to build you one of those nice timberframes. There's a building that can survive a tornado."

"We don't have tornadoes in Carniff County," she snapped.

Well, clearly I'd hurt her feelings, so I asked if she had any pictures of her new place, and she did.

The photograph shows a burly, bearded man in a

plaid flannel shirt. His lips are as straight as a pencil, and his eyes, hooded by the peak of his cap and heavy brows, are inaccessible. He's standing in front of the double-wide, next to a twelve-point buck hanging by its heels from a leafless tree in the yard. One possessive hand rests on the animal's antlers which are, like its tongue, and dark, open eyes, pointed at the ground. The other arm cradles his shotgun, a double-barreled beauty.

Shyly she showed me another picture of a pretty boy and girl and a black puppy almost bigger than the children. "That's Skeeter and Mikey, Jr.," she told me, "And Waldo the Wonderdog."

We shared a quick laugh over that, but then Esther lowered her voice. "Mike doesn't like Waldo," she said. "He says a gun-shy dog isn't worth a box of worms." She pushed a long wisp of hair behind her ear and the crisp lines at her mouth deepened. "But it's his own fault, Miss Irene. He shot over Waldo's head too soon, didn't get him used to sharp sounds first. My dad raised bird dogs. He would never have shot over a pup like Waldo."

"He might grow out of it, dear. I've had gun-shy collies that settled down, after a while," I lied.

"Anyway," she said, "That's my double-wide. What I'd really love to own is one of those new homes they're building over on Ridge Road. They're calling it Northridge Park and every house has a two-car garage."

I cringed as though she had slapped my face, but

I did not rebuke her. Esther disagrees with my conviction that these developments sprouting up like poison ivy are ruining this county, destroying the open fields and altering the beauty of my homeland forever.

Chapter Thirteen

ALL MY LIFE I PUT TAX MONEY IN THE BANK every month, always just a little afraid that someday there wouldn't be enough to keep my land. Every year the taxes rose, and every year I found just enough more money to keep my debts up-to-date.

It seems unfair. No one born and raised in this town has become wealthy, and unless they win that state gambling game, they never will be. Most people in these hills drive pickup trucks with jagged pieces of metal hanging from the fenders. Sometimes, because the men know how to fix things, they buy old equipment at a farm auction — a tractor, haybaler, or wagon — fix it up to use themselves, or re-sell at another auction for a little more money.

You can make some extra dollars that way, or from cutting and selling wood, or working on people's cars, maybe even selling some fresh eggs, but unless you have a huge farm you can't make money shipping milk anymore, and one or two hundred sheep won't pay the bills, either. Around here, small farming for a living has gone the way of blacksmiths and icemen, printers and coopersmiths, and doctors who come to the door.

Can it be that Esther is right? That old farmers like myself should slip away, vanish into a warehouse like Pine Manor? Should we get out of the way of our land, give it to the realtors? I see the Jim Sinclairs of the world lapping at the edges of rustic beauty, curiously poking at the serenity of the forests. Their tax forms are shaded with complexity; they turn over a leaf to study its underside and they see condominiums. I see something sinister that should be lanced like a boil and drained. But is this, as Esther says, "progress"?

Esther looked at me carefully. "You're a bit pale, Miss Irene," she said. "Are you tired?"

Frankly, I *was* tired and asked for a cup of tea. While she prepared the Lipton's, I settled back on the high pillows, thinking. Our conversation about the Northridge development had exhausted me. What if someone takes hold of my eighty-five acres and builds some dirty-named subdivision across the road from the Leahy cemetery?

AFTER LUNCH ESTHER SAID, "WOULD YOU like me to massage your hands, Miss Irene? It's good for the arthritis." She reached across the bed, stretching over me for the lotion.

"Good God, Esther," I yelped. "What is that?"

Too quickly she pulled the long sleeves of her cotton blouse back down to her wrist. "What?" she said.

"Why, those bruises. Did someone grab you?" I rolled the loose sleeve halfway up her arm and examined it. Ugly, yellow-tinged black and blue marks spread across her skin like a disease. I was shaking as I traced the shape of a hand, first on that arm, then on the other.

"What is this, Esther?" I asked.

She pulled away and laughed. "Those? You wouldn't believe what happened," she said, rolling down her sleeves. "I tripped and nearly fell down the stairs. Michael, my hero, caught me."

The only sounds were Esther's soft breathing and the rustle of bedclothes as she rubbed great globs of cream into my hands until they felt like warm and pliable wax. The bruises had been a shock to see, all right, but a troop of other smaller bruises and abrasions began to slowly march into my vision: the ones on the back of Esther's legs, the scrape along her jawline, and the three scratches on her neck, which I had attributed at the time to the sharp puppy claws of an untrained Waldo.

Esther smiled, "Close your eyes, now, Miss Irene." she said, and I did. But I had seen the photograph of Esther's single-story double-wide. Where were the stairs she said she had accidentally fallen down?

OLD PEOPLE LIKE MYSELF ARE VERY GOOD at smelling the truth. I can smell the Jim Sinclairs, lurking in the corners, buying and selling land. They are building little mountain lodge escapes with no regard for the howling winds that will blow right through their cheap facades, no sense of environmental unity or land usage. They neither know nor care that the moment a slice of land is sold, the earth is forfeited, irreversibly violated.

During the week, Sinclair goes back to work in the city. And now, on springtime weekends, when every bird is claiming its nest and preparing to multiply, he pleasures himself by shooting the crows. If I were a good Christian woman, I might warn him about that habit, but all I've done is register the activity in the sky over his place. Crows are the most intelligent of our native birds, even smarter than turkeys, and it is not an old wives' tale that they have a memory for evil acts against them. Shimmering iridescent black-purple, undulating in its feathers, the crow is the soul of the sky.

Whole tribes — two, three hundred strong — will stalk a farmer who has pointlessly dropped one of their own. They reconnoiter, congregating again — first two or three, then twenty or thirty, then eighty or a hundred. They sit high in the trees, a sea of cawing birds creating such a discordant hullabaloo that a certain melodious tone develops underneath the noise. They move through the air like southern-bound geese; attentive, focused, gathering on tree tops and telephone lines at intervals. They rest, take stock. Then, in a feathery sheet of black they fly low, glistening in the sun, locating their enemy, obsessively threatening to peck out the eye of the killer's barn cat or child, or dog, or wife.

I know that crows do this, for they did it to me when I shot one in my sweet corn. Mother was still alive and she panicked when she saw what I was doing.

"Irene, what is the matter with you?" she yelled at me. "Don't shoot at those birds. They'll hover, they will. They'll hover on you."

Well, I was a thirty-six-year-old woman who by then drove my own 1934 Chrysler and did not appreciate her tone of voice, which denied any possibility of a conversational reply. I knew what she was talking about, but the birds were eating our corn, and though Mother and I had learned to live together in reasonable peace, I had discovered ignoring her was an efficient tool.

The silence was like plate glass between us as Mother spent the rest of the day bent over the material of threadbare aprons, making scarecrows to put in the garden. Not until tin pie plates were replaced by modern aluminum was the crow problem temporarily licked. We strung the shiny lightweight tins on sticks and placed them in the garden. Noisily they whipped in the breeze, scaring the crows for a while, until inevitably they caught on and ignored the whole charade.

No matter how much corn they ate, I never brought the gun out against the birds again. In a useless act of desperation, I might have leapt out of the back door, yelling and waving my arms like a woman possessed, but only once does a flock of crows need to descend on my head.

Cityman Sinclair has probably never noticed the idiosyncrasies of a crow or a turtle, or luxuriated in the vision of fawns and does munching apples in the shadows. Urbanites with a polluted sense of nature are beginning to soil the landscape, and the trees of these northern woods are beginning to bend under the stress.

So am I.

Still, I must be fair and admit that one man alone cannot be blamed for the turning of the trees.

SINCLAIR IS RESPONSIBLE FOR THE SOUL OF one cat, though. I actually watched him kill her. It was about ten years ago, and a white cat was as asleep as the dead, curled in a sunspot right in the middle of the road. Flat as a pan on a coal stove, she was quite unaware that her life depended on me. I watched her anxiously, hoping she would move before a speeding car squashed her like a fuzzy bug.

Minutes passed. Nothing outside moved; no cars careened down Pike Road; no one pulled into the driveway. Finally I decided to save her myself. I pulled on an old sweater and headed out the front door.

It doesn't take a perfect pair of ears to identify the

vehicles around here. Levon Stiles's rusty Chevy has a high-pitched wheeze, Marty Lowell's chains have a peculiar pop to them, Patsy Garmondi's station wagon has its own cough, and my own blue pickup used to have brakes that squealed every time I turned a corner.

So I knew as I stood tottering on the front porch like an old fool, who was coming down the road, and he was driving more like an inexperienced teen-age boy than a graying businessman. I held onto the porch rail with both hands as Sinclair suddenly swerved into the middle of the rutted road. It was such a radical turn that at first I thought he'd lost control of the big Ford. But I suspected this man to be a character who seldom loses control, and I realized right away that he fully intended to run over that cat. After doing it, he stomped hard on the accelerator, throwing gravel and dust as if to celebrate the kill. He didn't even look in my direction.

The barn is usually full of cats this time of year. The feral ones have spent the winter living in the hay mows and by spring a litter has survived to take to the woods. A few months ago I heard the most forlorn wailing and I made Esther investigate. She grumbled; the March wind was fierce and I feared the barn would blow down around her, but just as I thought, she found a litter of seven newborn kittens. She said they were cuddled like balls of cotton in the manure spreader.

"Momma cat was dead, but looked to be sleeping,

content as could be," she told me. She had the grace not to mention it, but I know she went ahead and drowned them in the pond; there was nothing else for her to do.

I wish I could have walked down the hill to see them, but the exertion would probably have killed me, for I would also want to explore the old stalls and lambing pens. If I could stand there in the middle of the barn one more time, I would hear again the bawl of the lambs, and the sweet smell of the hay would tickle my nose.

Chapter Fourteen

IF SHE ASKED, I WOULD LET ESTHER READ a page or two of this journal, but she hasn't. Every day she comes, rustling about in the kitchen, sweeping the floor clean of Joe's dog hair and dead flies, and never does she mention my notebooks. It seems to me a studied inattention and that makes me suspicious. If she reads any of it, she must do it in proper sequence or she'll get the story all wrong.

But if Joe is any gauge, Esther can be trusted. He wags his tail as soon as she opens the screen door, and immediately the atmosphere is full of cheer. Of course, Joe now wags at Reverend Thorne, too, so maybe the old border collie is senile.

Today they took Joe for a walk while I was asleep, I found out. Perhaps they wandered slowly around the yard, Joe sniffing the lilac bushes, Esther and Reverend Thorne raising their faces to the sun. Then, because it's there, filled with remnants from the past, they walked down the hill to the barn the way I did so many years ago, effortlessly.

If I could go outside and walk into my barn again, I would put my hand on the old horse-drawn manure spreader — with its beaters and sprockets now frozen into flaking iron bones. The barn would vibrate again with the clanka-clanka-clanka of metal on metal, of the machinery I did not sell not only because no one wanted it, but also because the last person to touch it had been my father.

The old machinery was like a hand-made quilt; seemingly complicated but actually conceived on the couch of pattern and common sense. The horse-drawn spreader illustrates this as clearly as a fine pen and ink drawing. The design of today's spreader has scarcely changed since the days of the working horse. The narrow wooden carriage had three beaters to shred the manure and another horizontal spiral beater between the metal wheels. The team simply walked forward in front, moving a chain which pulled the manure through the spiral beater and out the back of the machine, spreading it onto the ground. The farmer's hardest work was shoveling the wet, heavy manure into the spreader, while the quizzical animals stood still in the barnyard and watched.

When my father worked the horses, his manly voice and the sound of the chains and conveyor belts made a certain kind of muffled music that echoed serenely throughout the hills. The horse-drawn machinery was quieter, and so much more tranquil, than the cacophony created by a modern tractor engine.

Gypsy and Pat were easy to drive. "Gee!" Father would thunder, commanding them to go right, or "haw!" to turn left. They lumbered along the field like spinster sisters, switching their tails, obediently working hard, unaware of the thick white foam that slathered around the heavy metal bits lodged in their mouths. They moved with an inner rhythm, sliding the handsawn logs that Father and Uncle Alton cut out of the woods.

These days I hear the new chain saws screaming like goats set for slaughter. It's true, some can make a living cutting wood, but it's a dangerous job. Every year an eager young man saws his face or hand or knee into two bloody flaps. And if they don't mangle themselves, they take their tractors and wood wagons into the forest, making deep muddy ruts, destroying the saplings, eroding the earth.

Skidding logs with his horses and managing his woodlot was Father's more rational way of cutting trees for heat. All year he studied them to determine which of the soft maples needed to be culled. Fall always signaled the beginning of the wood-gathering season, and every day until the job was done Mother packed a lunch for Father and Uncle Alton: hard bread and cheese, maybe some jerky and always a few apples. The satchel was bursting with food. Like weeding a gigantic garden, they would cut down the dispensable trees, opening the forest floor to sun, making space for the saplings to grow.

The first week they felled the trees, pushing and

pulling on the two-man saw. It was the kind of hard work a chainsaw operator never has seen, quiet and repetitive. It must have been gratifying work, for Father and Uncle Alton always looked forward to those brown and orange days in autumn when the geese pointed south.

The second week they spent pulling the trees out of the woods with Gypsy and Pat, placing them so that the third week could be used efficiently to cut the logs into burnable chunks. Ideally, by the end of October or definitely by Thanksgiving — no schedules can be relied upon when you're running on the slippery reality of a rural life — the wood was finally split, and Gypsy and Pat were again called to action.

They hauled wagon after wagon back down Pike Road to our woodshed until it bulged with firewood. The rest Uncle Alton sold. Like satisfied bears who have snuggled in for the winter, we all felt safe and prepared when the wood was neatly piled.

Every year offered a new set of wood-cutting tales. One time Gypsy was stung by a wasp while pulling a log to a clearing in the woods. She reared in panic and then collapsed, passed out in a tangle of leather and branches. Father said that she fainted, but I've never heard of a horse passing out. Whatever it was that happened, she revived quickly with no ill effects, stood up, shook herself all over, and commenced working, but it was lucky she didn't flail and fall on someone or break her own leg.

Most years were marked by some kind of break-down — wagon axles bending or wheels getting stuck in muddy ruts. One time, some of the Grange men came to help Father and Uncle Alton. Young Joe Phillips didn't keep his eyes open, and a widow-maker got him. The fat dead branch released its twisted grasp high in the arms of a maple tree and popped the boy hard on the head. He didn't bleed much, but was dizzy with headaches ever thereafter.

I myself never cut trees, or skidded logs with horses, or cut them into chunks of firewood. Hand saw or chain saw, horses or tractors, bringing in wood must be man's work for I've never seen a woman doing it.

Splitting and stacking was another story; how I loved those jobs.

WHEN I SOLD THE HORSES IN 1930, IT WAS with no ones blessings, not Uncle Alton's, certainly not my mother's.

"I think it's time to sell Gypsy and Pat, Mother," I said, a trifle brusquely, I now admit. It was an early summer evening and I'd been penciling our finances at my desk in the kitchen. "We need to get a tractor sooner or later and Ford is offering good rates at the bank in Wichner," I said.

My nose was buried in the books and not until she cried, "Absolutely not!" did I look up. I told her the truth. "I need the cash, Mother, not the horses. I don't want to winter them over, and you don't have to feed a tractor."

She glared at me in silence, then once more said, "No."

"We need to keep up, Mother. The world is changing fast. Look at this." I held up my latest copy of *Farm Life* and its full-page John Deere tractor advertisements. Tractor companies like Ford, International Harvester, John Deere and others were offering easy bank financing, even to tiny farms like mine.

With vicious speed she slapped the magazine out of my hands.

But I did sell Gypsy and Pat. One of the Amish farmers who came from the southern tier out of the Pennsylvania shadows offered me cash. Anyone could see that Gypsy and Pat were horses who had worked with the muscles of the gods, and as I turned them over to another farm, I concentrated on the knowledge that my decision was born of necessity and common sense.

There were 136,000 farms in all of New York State, and I wanted mine to be one of the 40,000 with a tractor. I am ashamed to admit it now, but I too wanted modern machinery in my barn, and a car in the carriage house more than I wanted the horses.

Mother, of course, had never once worked them, only Father and Alton and me. Like the modern hot rod shop or automotive repair, the town livery stable was not a place you would usually find a woman.

It was a place my mother would have blushed to walk into, for the language was as rough and tumble as the men. Yet I was a regular, and many times while I tended to the repair of harnesses or bought a needed wagon part, I stumbled into a secretive union of farmers who gathered together in a brotherhood of raw conversation. The oddly seductive perfume of horse manure and oiled leather, fresh hay and horse, seemed to cast a spell over us all, and I loved being able to join the men.

There wasn't too much to hitching Gypsy and Pat, though now I believe I've lost the knack. Still, many a farmer including my uncle, in a hurry to hitch up a piece of equipment, left a bloody finger out in the fields. Accidents occurred with the regularity of planting and harvesting, and while Uncle Alton was as helpful as he could be, I kept a steady eye on his activities. He was, you could say, an accident-prone man.

Even in these modern times it's usually men who lose their lives or limbs. At the whim of a rock or a stump, the tractor overturns, squashing them into the ground. Many are the times a man thinks he's almost finished with the day's haying. Tired to the bone and with visions of supper in his mind, he leaps into that split-second lapse of safety, and bales himself into one blood-soaked rectangle of hay, or forgets to take note of the slicing blades of the brush cutter.

A farmer's flesh cannot withstand more than one lapse of the brain, for these tragedies often occur in the field when he is alone and far away from help. How many farm wives have warmed up dinner, waiting anxiously to hear the weight of booted feet on the back door steps, the slam of the screen door?

Mother was distraught about the sale of Gypsy and Pat for a long time, and now that I am aged and wiser, I understand why. Father's strong "gee" and "haw" lived on in the muscles of the two beautiful creatures; they were the last vestige of her husband. Had I listened harder, I would have heard his voice myself, but my senses were dulled by practical matters.

THERE WAS A LIGHT-HEADED PERIOD, JUST before I sold the horses, when a rosebush I had planted on Billy's grave began to bloom. Summer honeybees tickled its miniature white flowers, which skipped and giggled like children. I began to muse about my brother, about his lonely, avoidable death.

I spoke to no one about it, but the idea of Billy followed me like a sweet, unidentifiable smell. My sheep were thriving, the farm was solvent and I was responsible for it all. The only man in my world was quirky Uncle Alton, who seemed destined to odd twists of fate, and whose appetite for amusement outweighed his common sense. I loved my uncle — he could shear a ram faster than my father — but he, like many men confused by war and poverty and the steady muscle-straining labor that always accompanies outdoor work, often failed to observe the basic social rules. Sometimes his bathing habits wrinkled my nose; sometimes his ribaldry landed him a black eye.

One unexceptional day when I was hiring some men to help with the shearing, I had the odd notion that a tall, grown-up Billy, blonde as cornsilk and angelically handsome, was standing next to me. When I spoke, it seemed that my words were not my own, but Billy's. The men I hired were speaking to me through him, and later that week it happened again when I decided to build a new barn. Billy helped me hire the carpenters and negotiate the price.

For exactly one month, until the day Gypsy and Pat were hauled away, when I assigned the day's chores to the farmhands, or made a risky business decision, it was with an eerie certainty that Billy was next to me. Now I know what he was doing there, that the reason he appeared was to save Gypsy and Pat. Because from the moment those horses left the farm, I never had the feeling he was near me again.

He was a desperate messenger. "Let the horses die in peace, Reeni, on the ground where we were all born and raised." He was asking me to listen, and as usual, I did not.

Chapter Fifteen

THE AUGUST 3, 1937 ISSUE OF *THE FARM
Journal* printed an article under the headline "Leahy
Rams are Superior." Everyone in the sheep business
knew my name, and most, I presume, knew that the
Leahy sheep farm was managed by a single woman.
After all, there I was on the front cover, sitting
up on my new tractor in patched, baggy dungarees
and a red flannel shirt, with wisps of hair sneaking
out of my uncle's fishing hat. Maybe I was a spinster and not quite the cover girl some magazines
would choose, but my thirty-seven-year-old smile
was healthy and I was robust. In the background was
my champion flock of Dorsets hanging like white
clouds in grass so pastoral even I could not believe it.

The magazine made quite a splash here in
Donohue Flats. Everyone bought a copy and Mr.
Delaney, the postmaster, even asked me to autograph
the cover.

"You're the biggest celebrity this side of Wichner,"

he joked. "Even the new veterinarian was asking about you."

In the immediate way people who cherish their privacy react to such statements, my back stiffened and I looked up from the farm girl on the magazine cover. "What do you mean? What's he want to know about me?"

"Now don't get your knickers in a twist. He saw the magazine article and was interested in your sheep."

"Well if you see him again," I said slowly, remembering the man I'd noticed a few days earlier at the General Store, "Tell him I said he's welcome to come see my sheep."

Maxwell Hunter and I hadn't spoken that day but at the time I did notice how attractive he was, mature with white streaks in his clipped full beard, and an air of confidence which made him seem more handsome than he actually was. Always confused by romantic matters, inept at flirtation, bemused by attention, I was an unmarried woman who kept my own gates. I was more skillful in affairs of business, and earlier than I anticipated, my procreative door slammed shut. Choice and circumstance were equally responsible, and with a heavy helping of self-preservation donated by my mother, I had no time or desire to reveal myself to strange men.

Yet the new veterinarian's easy smile had begun to follow me as I went about my day, nagging me into thoughts that made me blush.

Cooking, laundering, sewing, all of these were

steady and predictable chores, and while I did them all, I was more proficient at slopping hogs, tending chickens, and doctoring lambs. Perhaps if Billy had lived, my natural inclination to men's work would have been discouraged, but my mother's own survival instinct was quite high. She knew her limits, but in a perfect world, one with a live husband and son, I think her daughter would have learned to dance with boys and flirt with men.

Dancing.

Dancing never appealed to me like it did the other town girls, and I never learned to do it very well. They kicked their heels with skirts flashing in a circle of color at the square dances the Grange held in our town hall. I was too bashful for that, but once a month while I cut the homemade pies and poured the tea, my toes would tap to the good country music Uncle Alton and his ragtag friends used to make — fiddles and banjoes, mouth harps and song.

I found myself daydreaming about those dances of my youth and the boys who rarely sought my attention. Every night at sunset, after supper and before darkness fell, I wandered to the edge of the pond where I watched the reflection of clouds moving across the water. I imagined adroitly following Maxwell Hunter's steps, and then, breathless and laughing, leaning against him when the music stopped. And I imagined myself young and pretty, a different woman.

Most of the girls I knew back when we were all

inexperienced and fresh-faced were desperate to escape their life in the country. My friend Penny was one of them. Armed with a typing certificate and high school diploma, she left town as soon as she could. Threw away her wool cap and sunbonnet in favor of a veiled and flowered hat. The minute she was old enough to leave Carniff County she was on her way. Left the predictable dairy farm to find a man unlike her father, one who did not wear overalls; one with a car instead of a horse who would provide her with a brick house on a hard road, not a rutted dirt path and white clapboard shack.

The last time I saw Penny was at her father's auction. Mr. Dalton had been a good dairyman. He produced the most milk in the county with the highest butterfat, but the mastitis destroyed his farm like a cannonball through a wooden ship's bow. He retired, telling anyone who would listen that "he was sick and tired of teats." Penny, all dolled up in a big hat and high heels, and her fat banker husband showed up with a moving van to take anything of value back to New York City.

I can't explain why desires like Penny's never presented themselves to me. Nothing could drive me from my home, not apple blossoms in Paris, not musicals in New York, not promises of men who would polish me up and set me on a mantel. There were a few boys, of course.

Luther Campbell once spit out his chaw and kissed me on the mouth, and there was a barnraising where a boy whose name I cannot recall told me that he thought I was pretty. When I asked Mother to have him for supper, she refused on the spot.

"No Donohue Flats boy is going to court you, Reeni." She smiled. "They don't want you, they want the farm." And because I was sure my mother had never lied to me before, I believed her.

In the end, the solitary life that started so early fit me like a warm wool mitten. Loneliness has been as foreign to me as Chinese food. My family has been lambs and piglets, calves, goats and foals, chicks, puppies, kittens and other wild beasts — coons and possum, chipmunks and squirrels have been my offspring. The vegetable garden was my passion and a generation of fruit and nut trees still thrive on the land I tilled. The milk and maple syrup, the flowers and golden honey, for a taste of these things I traded colorless time.

I can close my eyes now and I am a young woman extracting honey from the combs of my beehive. It drips thickly from my elbows and I suck my sweet fingers dry. Sometimes the healthy smell of a newly delivered lamb, the sticky afterbirth steaming on the hay, rises like smoke above my bed and I am in the barn, clearing the newborn's wet nose, anxious to see it suckle. Yes, I close my eyes and inhale, and the years left in my life are still high in number.

If I am to be honest, I must admit to the occasional sleepless night when a wandering mind asks answerless questions. What kind of wife might I have made Dr. Maxwell Hunter? What kind of mother to his children? And what kind of sister, too, I wonder. Surely Billy would have married and given me nieces and nephews, a family to protect this lonely old farm.

Chapter Sixteen

THERE WAS A TIME WHEN MY BODY WAS
sturdy like a rosebush, not reedy and weak like a single stem. I long for those robust days pilfered by life and by time. On glorious summer days while Mother cooked and cleaned and canned tomatoes, I worked as long and hard as any man. Stringing fence, pulling the barbed wire from one locust pole to the next, to the next, to the next, until the leather of my gloves was sliced and ruined, my face sun blistered and red, sweat rolling like rain down my back. Resting, gulping water from a jug of fresh spring water, my breath was clear and deep and joyful.

And then in winter, while Mother repaired splits in my dungarees and holes in my socks, I sweat again. Chipping at the pond frozen as thick as the length of my arm, finally the pick would defeat the ice, passing through it like a ghost through a wall. The impossibly cold water splashed up in my face and my muscles grew hard as I dipped buckets to take to the sheep.

My body was once as reliable as a sailor's knot, but now it's slack and unraveled. The journey to disintegration can be arduous; I am as weightless as a spider's web but just as tenacious.

Esther may not be strapping, but she is from farm stock, and beneath her slight frame is a woman as strong as a bantam-weight boxer. It is not muscle she lacks, but confidence. Even though she moves about my house in efficient spurts, vacuuming the floor, dusting the furniture, resting now and then with a cup of coffee, I sometimes see her hands shake. And when she bends at the waist to feed old Joe, who these days greets his kibble with little interest, she does so quickly, as if the position is risky.

Joe was once like Molly, full of vigilance and passion but he was made gun-shy, and there's not much a person can do to ease the worries of such a dog. He was less than a year old, still a rough and tumble pup, when that McCrady boy squealed his rusty truck to a halt at the top of the hill. It was mid-summer and I was collecting ferns in the woods to transplant to my little perennial garden, when I heard the gravel fly. It sounded like an emergency stop, so I hurried right out of the shady forest.

Joe pranced along in front of me, snorting every woodchuck hole in his path. He does remind me of Molly — I'm talking coat and eyes — but after this day you could never depend on the dog to bring in a whole flock of sheep. Now, a backfiring car will freeze him in his tracks, and target practice down in the valley turns him to a quivering black and white hump.

Just as we walked over the knoll at the far end of the field, the young driver in a yellow shirt jumped out of the truck and pointed a shotgun at the back of a fat woodchuck. The muzzle glinted in the afternoon sun and while I have no use for woodchucks — their holes will murder your machinery — it was unlawful for a stranger to shoot across a farmer's land.

A woodchuck is a winsome little animal. Self-contained and funny to watch, he wreaks havoc in a patch of lettuce and the tunnels he digs in a hayfield can cause a tractor to roll. This chuck sat up like a cartoon grizzly about fifty yards in front of me. Clearly, the yellow-shirted interloper intended to shoot it, an animal who, by virtue of residence, belonged to me. True, on another day, I might have shot the rodent myself, but this day I was ready to intercede.

Apparently so intent on this fabricated sport that he failed to see me, the boy squeezed the trigger twice before the woodchuck ambled back to his hole. I stumbled across the field toward the road, swinging my cane and shouting. I wanted to pull that young man up by his dirty ears and thrash him with a stick, but he climbed back into his truck and sped away, cheerfully spitting dust and gravel. Irreversible damage happens fast and this one boneheaded act affected my dog for the rest of our lives.

He was yelping, crouched close to the ground as if he'd been shot. I saw him slink into the woods like a sheep-eating coyote. Border collies are intelligent dogs and more sensitive than most, but when those shots blasted, Joe disappeared like a mosquito at noon. It took me the rest of the afternoon to find him, huddled behind a hollow log. His teeth were chattering. The joy he should have had from racing free was, like his serenity, gone forever. We were both scarred and swindled, and when I saw the terror in his glazed eyes and the blood dripping slowly from his rear leg onto the mossy carpet, I promised to keep him safe from that day on.

Many are the nights I've cursed that boy and his brainless act, for even though age has taken Joe's sense of hearing, the wizardry of his breed remains. Hours before a storm is upon us, the dog abandons his blanket behind the stove in the kitchen, begins to pace and pant and drool. He senses the thunder, associating it with the sound of a booming gun, and though he cannot hear it, the lightning warns him that it's coming. He hides under my bed, whining and shaking, ruining a good night's sleep for both of us.

I should make him sleep in the barn, but he would not feel safe and I would be breaking my promise. Each morning we wake, functioning poorly. I scratch his salt and pepper muzzle and he licks my misshapen hands, congratulations proffered to each other for witnessing another day.

I made arrangements for Joe when he was about

ten years old. Even though he was still as sprightly as an auctioneer, I was not. I instructed the Grange women to make sure somebody shoots the dog and buries him up on the hill next to Molly. "Do this the same day I'm buried," I said, but I can't be sure they will.

Frankly, I didn't expect to live this long, but Joe has decided to be my very last dog and I can tell he's tired after fourteen years. I just hope he dies before I do. They say dogs do not grieve or mourn, but they are wrong. Like I said before, Joe's blood is mingled with the blood of the finest border collie that ever lived and Molly mourned my father. Oh yes, dogs do mourn.

TODAY ESTHER HUSTLED INTO THE HOUSE like a young puppy. "Happy June first, Miss Leahy! I spotted these flowers on the way over this morning. Aren't they pretty? I'll go ahead and put them in a vase for you."

Her eyes, shiny dark nuts behind her glasses, danced behind the stems of the Queen Anne's lace and musk mallows. I studied her face carefully and she does have the look of June today. The promise of summer can do wonders for a complexion, but the eyes do not lie and hers are lit, I think, only temporarily.

"Michael brought me flowers last night," she said, shyly, and looked away. "We've been arguing a bit

116

lately, but he really wants to make me happy. He gave me a huge bouquet of real florist flowers. When I saw these alongside the road this morning, I thought of you and how it might be nice if someone gave you flowers, too."

She seemed so pleased that I held my tongue. I didn't tell her some flowers are best left alone. Some flowers, especially those that grow in fields or next to clear meandering streams in the woods, are not meant to come indoors. Some flowers, for heaven's sake, should remain undisturbed, left to jiggle and bob on their courageously slender stems. Those proud pink and white musk mallows that so filled her arms this morning will be flaccid as used paper straws by this afternoon.

"Can I use this vase, Miss Irene?" Esther asked, stretching to her full height to reach the top pantry shelf. The flowers were already wilting, but I let her do it, hoping they wouldn't make my eyes water.

Mother had never allowed flowers in the house. One time, on the way home from Penny's house, I picked an armful of daisies and Queen Anne's lace. It was a long dusty walk from her farm to mine, a hot sunny day, and the flowers were droopy by the time Molly and I walked in the back door.

Mother was furious, her face wet and red. She had just chased a fox out of the henhouse and clearly could have used my help. Perspiration leaked down the collar of her house dress and a few downy feathers were pasted like white curls on her neck.

"Don't bring those weeds in here, Reeni," she snapped, grabbing the bouquet. "You know what they do to me."

She threw the whole load outside as if they were hot coals. Penny's mother always kept a big vase of flowers on her kitchen table, and I guess I'd forgotten that my mother was allergic to pollen. Calmer, she told me something that made sense.

"Flowers are meant to live outside like the birds, Reeni."

It was a house rule I eventually adopted because right then and there I myself started to sneeze, my nose dripping like an icicle hanging in the sun.

The bouquet that sits in a farm wife's kitchen is a hindrance to nature. It's hard to believe we share such a delicate balance, but it's true. Bees can't hover above the bloom, diving deep into the petals to pack their elbows with tiny powder puffs of golden pollen. Butterflies must search for another fountain of nectar. We must choose our violations carefully.

Until my body defied me, every April I walked the floor of the woods, looking for the new season's first flower. She's a dainty little thing, the "spring beauty." A small star less than an inch across, she is early evidence that another upstate New York winter has ungraciously yielded. Rosepink pinstripes decorate her white, delicate petals. Lying low to the ground in iridescent clusters, she doggedly pushes her head through the leathery mats of snow-smashed leaves. But announcing the end of winter is not her only act, for tied to her feet are tiny edible tubers; sweet little potatoes.

My mother, whose own mother died giving birth to her tenth child, learned of necessity and taught me at an early age that the woods are a diner. "There is so much to eat out here," she told me, "That even without a vegetable garden, it would be hard to starve. Look, Reeni," she said, pointing to what looked like a soft white grapefruit lying in the grass.

She picked the meaty fungus and dropped it in a satchel. "We called this a puffball when I was a girl. We'll slice it and fry it for supper tonight, just so you can taste."

So I could taste, we also gathered unfolding fronds that grow from the center of fiddlehead ferns. From those, she made a creamy soup, and from the bright green cowslip, which grew like seaweed in a swampy spot across the road, she boiled up kale-like greens. But cowslip is a spring dish, and when its sunny yellow flowers bloom in August, the leaves are too tough and bitter to eat.

It's a curious element of our nature that people tend to seek the rare, and ignore the common. Thus the comical skunk cabbage and common ferns, wild iris and violets that erupt in an early spring forest seem wan and ordinary compared to some of the other wildflowers. Mother showed me all of them: Dutchman's breeches, Indian pipe, squirrel corn, and fireweed. Ginseng, Jack-in-the-pulpit, trillium, daisy flea bane, Queen Anne's lace, yarrow, and coreopsis. Touch-me-not, lady's slipper, mullein, goldenrod, day lily, and the vivid blue New York aster. Sumac, dock, bull thistle, bee balm, dwarf iris, pokeweed, and Indian paintbrush.

"All of our soothing ointments, killing potions, nutritious edibles and tonics, and noxious poisons, come right out of these woods, Reeni," she said. "The secrets of good and evil reside here."

I've never forgotten that lesson. Just two feet off of the road lies a staggering universe full of solutions to modern puzzles. People listen to the radio as they drive past the answers.

Chapter Seventeen

SUMMER PASSES SWIFTLY IN CENTRAL NEW
York. By June, everything is in motion. Jim Sinclair
comes up more often, spending long weekends away
from the city. At night, for recreation, he rides slowly
up and down Pike Road, shining a flashlight out of
the car window, searching the fields. The pale amber
eyes of the springborn fawns are frozen in the light,
and Sinclair is assured of another hunting season in
the fall.

I'll be the first to admit that deer can decimate a
garden, and I don't complain about hunters, as long
as they abide by two rules. Stay off of my land: I don't
want bullets raging through my kitchen. Over in New
Binford someone shot a refrigerator, for heaven's
sake. And eat the meat. I say too many people are
hungry to let a venison roast go to waste.

I'm told that expensively mounted deer heads decorate Sinclair's house and he has a collection of antlers nailed to the empty dairy barn. Each year they
bleach whiter and increase in number. He keeps no
animals, doesn't eat a bit of the meat he hunts. Now,

121

if I were God, that is something I would call a sin. Seems to me that killing animals for recreation ought to be right up there with lust and greed. Sinclair wastes his time, searching for next year's trophies. This time of year he'd be better off gardening.

By now, he could have planted all of the seeds and bulbs in the black, anxious soil. The garden is poised to produce. Imperceptibly the gritty earth begins to shift. Pale green tendrils break through the tiny seed walls and spidery vines reach to the sky. Crystal-line grains of earth stretch, changing position. Seeds tumble and roll in the dirt. Hibernating cells of life awaken and develop; food occurs, no blood spilt.

TODAY, AFTER ESTHER ARRANGED THE flowers she brought me on the kitchen table, she opened the windows for the summer and vacuumed the screens. I can see the topheavy Queen Anne's Lace leaning against the peeling white fence in front of the house and the bright dandelions nesting like egg yolks in the yard, obscuring the ugliness. I can smell June, hear its noisy chirp and buzz. Clouds of birds trill at each other, meeting in the sky in a flash of brilliance, swooping and screaming, then resting like painted ornaments on the highest cattails in the pond.

Esther intentionally raises her voice now, as if I was altogether deaf, which I am not. "You don't have to scream, dear," I say to her, but she continues blaring in my ear as if I'm the one with the problem.

Sometimes I'm as glad to see Esther as I am to see a good, full-blown rainbow. But this is not always so. When a stranger crosses into your bedroom, touches your cosmetics and your comb, sees the brand of lotions and medications on your bureau, you've entered into a world without privacy.

I wonder if Esther is reading my notebooks now, prying into pages when I sleep, pencil still in my hand. She might be looking at every word I write on this lined paper, this blotter that sucks the fluid of my memory dry.

Sometimes I can't recall exactly how she came into my life. I didn't hire her myself, Reverend Thorne didn't. How do I know she's not a natural busybody, poking her nose into other people's business? I see her as she walks back from the mailbox, looking over my letters as if we were family. This Esther Pomeroy may try to treat me like family, bringing me groceries and gifts, sharing photos of her own family with me, but she is not.

Look how she brought those weeds into the house, those pale pink and white musk mallows that are already wilting in the Mason jar on the kitchen table. They are going to make me sneeze my nose off, and my congested lungs will fall weak like tissue and I will be afraid to breathe. If those flowers bother me, I will write a letter, I will. I will tell the social services that this Esther Pomeroy is bad and that she is invading my privacy and reading my mail. I will tell them that she and Reverend Thorne are conspiring against me, which I know they are. They take walks together, with my dog, planning how to move me to Pine Manor.

The bruises on Esther's arms are fading, I notice. I expect there will be others.

She can be aggravating, the way she studies each piece of my mail as if she thinks *her* name might be printed on the envelopes. Most of my mail is circulars and bills, but I do get a scribbly handwritten letter now and again, like the one from a blood relative, a *real* relative. I asked Esther to read it to me; she has such a lovely reading voice:

Dear Miss Irene Leahy,

It's been a long time since last I wrote to you. Hope you are feeling well. I've been laid up with a back sprain for many weeks but otherwise have been okay. The dairy farmer I work for, Mr. Addisson, has been kind and provides me with a trailer. I do all of the milking and keep the cows in good shape. I put flowers on Kathleen's grave last Memorial Day. Take good care of yourself.

Best Regards,
Jerome Anderson

The trouble is that this Jerome Anderson never writes his return address on the envelope. I am not sure exactly how I am related to him.

I GET SOME CHRISTMAS CARDS, TOO, though I don't send them out anymore. The

Turtle Brand Oil Company sends one every year, a printed card with no sign of a human touch. I put it on the mantel, but I don't send one back.

All the years with Mother and Father, and then all the years until I got a television, I never felt lonely during the Christmas holidays. But after the events of that black November in 1963, I went out and bought an RCA. I didn't want to become as stubborn and old-fashioned as my mother, who predicted that television would unravel the world. I must have been the only American alive who didn't see Lee Harvey Oswald get his comeuppance, but I didn't miss the very first moonwalk. I refuse to close my eyes to history.

There is something eerie about those TV images, though. They're always laughing and dancing and having a much better time than anyone deserves. I wonder if my own memories have been transformed by them. Was that my father trudging a path through the snow on Christmas Eve to cut the biggest spruce we could find? Or am I remembering a Christmas special?

He would set it up in the corner of the parlor and Mother and I would wrap it with strings of popcorn for decoration. We cut strips of colored paper and made a long chain of rings to drape around the tree. The fresh scent of pine drifted throughout the house and sometimes an abandoned bird's nest would be hidden in its branches.

Fire blazing, Father would slip in the back door

and surprise us with baskets of oranges and candy. Mother got a fresh new apron every year and a handkerchief. I got handmade wooden toys or dolls until I was old enough to ask for books. Christmas was the one day of the year that we dressed up, put red ribbons on Gypsy and Pat, hitched them to the cutter and went to church together.

When I lived alone, I continued to cut my own tree, which each Christmas became smaller and easier to handle. But a few years ago, I bought a lovely little permanent tree at the Grange bake sale and bazaar on Election Day. Everyone comes to vote, and most of the baked goods are sold by noon. I was the first to spot the green ceramic tree. It was perched on the sale table, a shiny sample of someone's hobby.

Well, I plunked down $3.50 in Kennedy half dollars, which happened to be weighing down my pocket because I'd just sold four dozen eggs to Ralph Hart. He liked to pay in silver. I was lucky to get the tree because that year a record 621 people turned out to vote. I don't remember what the fuss was all about, but the town was steamed that election year.

The tree was electrified with colored lights inside and I found out when I got it safely home that it was also a music box! I can hear "God Rest Ye Merry, Gentlemen" as often as I like. I wouldn't mind keeping the thing on the oak plant stand in the parlor all the time. Every year I wait longer and longer to pack it away, and last year Esther finally did it for me sometime in March, I think. I miss it.

But here it is the magnificent month of June. Why do I contemplate Christmas and the sunless winter? Perhaps it is because of Jim Sinclair. Summertime brings him out.

For people like Sinclair, winter is inconvenience and worry about frozen water pipes and slippery roads. They come here to escape the crowded city life, then try to escape again to a warmer climate. Those rich golden autumns and emerald springs that flank the lean white winter months are merely pages to turn on a calendar. When naked ice queens sail the merciless winds, howling and navigating the mountain peaks and the valleys, the Jim Sinclairs sink into their newspapers. They look away from the full face of the moon, are blind to the beauty of the seasons that sparkle with the brief and fragile perfection of a new mother's eyes. In winter, especially, there are cracks in time, irretrievable split seconds when the future is released and the frozen cloak fades. The Jim Sinclairs panic and burrow deeper into their bottles of scotch.

THE FLOWERS HAVE NOT YET MADE ME sneeze. Their musky scent is subtle like the smell of my father's lanolin-stained hands or the starch of Mother's house dress.

When Esther goes home this afternoon, I'll get out

of this bed. I'll be careful to keep my balance until I'm safely in my walker. Then I'll throw the spent and short-lived bouquet away. I don't want to hurt Esther's feelings, for she has been very gentle today, washing my laughable hair, combing it softly so as not to hurt my scalp, and she did not mention Pine Manor one time.

My father and mother were luckier than me. His short life was pinched out like a candle flame, and he never knew the humiliation of having a stranger comb his hair or wash his back. Mother's luck was different. After her stroke, when she dribbled food out of her twisted face, I was there to help her. I fed her, scrubbed her chicken skin, clipped her blue nails. But nowadays there's no guarantee your children will take care of you. I know this to be true because I can count the number of Grange women whose sons and daughters winter in Florida, summer in the Adirondacks. Truth is no one really wants to touch someone else's privates, even if there is money involved.

Knowing this, I appreciate my Esther. Only when my mind plays tricks on me do I doubt her. In old age, confusion is a brutal enemy. I know I am her job, her charge, her paycheck, but we do chat, and I think she likes to talk to me because it transports her away, like my journals transport me. I wish she could stay with me all the time, the way I stayed with my mother.

Usually, she is as rushed as a firefighter to get

home to her children, but today she was not anxious to leave. Today she dawdled, needlessly dusting polished furniture, watering the watered African violets. Finally she said brightly, "Your hair will mat like wet leaves if we don't brush it out before I go home."

"But Esther, dear," I said, "Michael must be expecting you home soon?"

She picked up the brush and began to work on my hair without comment. My Esther is not so stupid after all. She distrusts Michael's peace offering as much I do.

I aimed the conversation in another direction. "Do you have a garden, Esther?" I asked. "You should be planting lettuce and carrots now, and your peas and onions are already in, aren't they? Come August you'll have plenty of work to do, what with all of the canning."

She brushed my hair, working out the tangles, which come from I don't know where.

"I don't do much canning myself, Miss Irene, just applesauce for Michael," she said. "My mother used to put up all kinds of fruits and vegetables, though. I can almost taste the pickles. I don't know how she did it, to tell the truth. I had four younger brothers and Mom worked right next to Dad milking thirty cows."

"Well, I've canned everything there is," I told her. "Every fruit and vegetable, meat and sauce. Then when I bought that half-size Sears freezer back there in the pantry, I went to freezing. But I never gave up canning altogether. Found out some things just don't freeze well, and there's nothing better than a little canned chicken stew."

"Did you have a root cellar? I think we had one."

"Probably you did. Most of the farm houses had a root cellar where we kept baskets of carrots and beets, potatoes and turnips. All of the root crops and apples, too. Always had enough to eat, even during the Depression."

We fell silent. From its constant contact with my pillow, the hair on the back of my head snarls like steel wool. It takes a patient hand, but my own patience was lacking.

"Aren't you finished fooling with my hair yet, Esther?"

"Not quite yet."

"Well, my neck hurts. Will you get me some tea? I need a rest."

While she prepared the Lipton's, I settled back on the bed, thinking. The bruises on her sleeveless arms were discolored blotches now, but I could still see an outline of fingerprints. Sometimes I'm afraid I say too much to this girl. She gets me to talking and I forget what I told her.

Have I asked her to come to live with me?

I MUST HAVE DOZED, BECAUSE WHEN Esther returned with a plate of Fig Newtons, a teapot, and two of my delicate china cups, I jerked like a skittish colt. There in front of me was Reverend Thorne, standing at the foot of the bed like an awkward little boy, baseball hat in hand, Bermuda shorts and green tee shirt hanging on his bony frame like clothes on a line. He smiled in a way that made me stare, for I'd seen that smile before and I knew where I could go to see it again.

It is becoming more urgent that I go to the attic. The reasons are piling on top of one another, spilling all over like a bowl of popcorn in a child's lap.

For one thing, I must find my photograph albums. I will linger over the pictures, carefully turning each fragile, age-cracked page. In those brittle books I will find many smiling images of Maxwell Hunter, some with his protective arm around me, some of me gazing up at him, mature and dangerously in love.

Reverend Thorne's smile — his straight teeth and the line of his lips with their softly uplifted corners — is identical to Max's. Why have I never noticed that before?

Chapter Eighteen

B<small>Y</small> SEPTEMBER OF 1937, I HAD ALREADY outlived George Gershwin, Amelia Earhart, my own father, and half of the year's lamb crop. Five lifeless lambs were piled outside the barn door like a mound of dirty wool sweaters. Most of the thirty live ones left staggered unsteadily in the pen. It was a fast-moving sickness, spreading among the lambs from nose to nose.

Oddly, the ewes did not seem to be infected, but I was worried nonetheless. After the August article featuring my sheep farm in *The Farm Journal*, I did not want any bad publicity to ruin my reputation. One by one, I carried the healthy lambs into a hastily constructed isolation pen at the far end of the barn. The adolescent lambs wriggled in my arms, twisting, kicking, intent on a bouncing frolic in the hay.

Almost insolently, the afflicted animals stood still, staring at the barn walls with disinterest. They moved only to cough or ineffectually toss their heads to clear the yellow string of thick mucus that flowed from their noses. Pupils dilated the size of large black buttons, the sick lambs snorted and hacked like a roomful of consumptive old men.

That day, I did not lean out of the paneless barn window to watch the flaming sunset, but stood in the middle of the pen, studying the animals. The barn seemed wet and humid despite the strips of peach light seeping through knotholes and slits in the siding. Hay dust percolated in the early evening light and the ailing lambs sneezed uncontrollably.

The barn never did have glass in its panes. Mother insisted that to close out the winter air would bring on disease. "Cold kills the germs," she said. "And sheep like a little snow against their lips."

But this was an unusually steamy week in September and the animals should have been outside. The fence should have been repaired more than a month ago, but Uncle Alton had been kicked in the thigh by a horse and the farm work had been delayed.

Now, this. Sick lambs. I was already exhausted. Each pitiful bleat of the dying animals cracked against the inside of my skull like a whip.

A brass band of realities slowly marched behind my eyes. Amelia had vanished without a trace over the Pacific. And Roosevelt barked from our radio that one-third of the nation was ill-housed, ill-clothed, ill-nourished. Gershwin, just one year older than I was, died suddenly at thirty-eight. But more distressing than all of this was an uneasy knowledge that someone named Hitler was going to cause everyone trouble, lots of it.

On top of everything else, I couldn't forget what I'd overheard at the general store. Gossipy Viola Peabody and Helen Nutley didn't see me come in, and I heard just the last part of their conversation:

". . . Irene is quite the shepherd, I suppose, but what's an old maid like that going to do when her mother dies and she has no one?"

I had never before linked the words "old maid" to myself, and as I stood motionless in the isolation pen, hunched against one of the twelve-by-twelve posts that supported the framework of the barn, I began to think of Maxwell Hunter, the vet.

Slowly the healthy sheep, still behaving normally, curiously gathered at my feet. They nudged my legs, pushed their noses into my hands searching for a salty lick. Then drifting away, calm and acquiescent, they lay down in the hay to chew their cud. I was anchored to the spot; this barn was the center of the universe, a cozy haven. The dank smell of dung and lanolin and animal breath mingled to swirl in my nostrils like thick sweet-burning incense.

Suddenly the future seemed dry as drought, predictable and ominous. Fears rushed in my head, swirled like sand in a storm. My knees could not take the strain and folded under me.

Briefly, I sought the soft pearl light of reason, but my mental strength had drained away. The barn was too comfortable, too willing to indulge my conceit. I allowed the black velvet cape to fall over my shoulders, and sank to the hay-cushioned floor.

My veins dried like burning grass into crisp tendrils, tightening around my bones. Violent patterns zigzagged behind my closed eyes. A searing heat seemed to bubble the skin on my face like burning paint.

When finally I opened my dry eyes, they were pasted on the wooden pegged barn ceiling and I was on my back flat on the animal bedding. I was not afraid, not even of the blood that was streaming from my nose. Hay and dung balls hung from my hair. The sheep took turns defensively squatting and peeing, and wet patches soaked my knees as I searched the bedding for my buried eyeglasses.

My fingers pushed aside piles of shiny black marbles. It was a good sign, these hard little balls of manure, for when sheep leave soft puddles, they may have overeaten. Like goats and cows, they are ruminants with no self-regulation. Prone to breaking into the feed bag, they will dine themselves into an internal gas explosion.

But I was as sick as the lambs myself that day, and there would be no quick fix. Dizzy, I fell back into the smelly, sodden hay and studied the ceiling of the barn, trying to collect myself. The walls were luminous as if freshly whitewashed. The mortise and tenon joints and pegs were strong, built to last generations.

Many of the old rust-red post and beam barns are still standing here in the northeast, because someone during the past one hundred and fifty years took the time to repair and maintain the hand-hewn beasts. There are many more dilapidated examples of disrepair — sad, black skeletal remains of the wooden barns teetering on crumbled foundations. Each winter the roofs sink a little deeper under the snow load. Every blast of wind peels another board or shingle. Finally its spine is broken and the barn cracks, then collapses.

I felt as splintered and fallen as those old barns and as I stared at the stripped logs and hand-notched posts, my wheezy breath matched that of the sheeps'. The years of shepherding had taught me to move like a ewe, maybe even to think like one. I rested with them, waiting, inhaling the barn air in deep, quiet gulps.

Gradually the pounding in my ears subsided and the pain went away, but I was in no hurry to stand. As snug as a nun in a cathedral, I studied the ten-foot maple posts. They were pegged into four twenty-two-foot frame beams. Thin strips of bark from the one-hundred-year-old trees were still attached, and the hewn marks of labor were as deep as the lines in a hard worker's hand. I watched the clean adze marks in the beams above me, expecting another strike.

The background nickers of the ewes and their lambs grew more intense as a new hot wave coursed from the bottoms of my feet up to the roots of my hair. A queasy compulsion to stand interrupted my meditation and the sheep were suddenly noisily bleating.

Bleating, bleating, bleating.

My head split like a shucked oyster, and I was in trouble again. I held my hands tight against my ears. Another smaller sound traveled toward me. Like the whistle of a night train at the far end of a long tunnel, it came closer and closer.

Suddenly it passed and my eyes opened cautiously. On my right was Mother, kneeling over me as if in prayer. From the middle of the hazy faint, I can see her face looking down at me, so close to mine that I dreamily thought I was looking into a cracked hand mirror. It is a watery reflection of my own with lips that look swollen as they mouth my name.

On my left, as tall as a water tower, stood someone else. It took some minutes before I realized the figure was not imaginary; it was a man. At first I irrationally thought he was the German immigrant who had built our house and barn, the man whose muscles breathed life into this uncleared land that came to be my farm.

I squinted. This man gazing down at me was rugged, with a barrel chest and thick arms. Dark-skinned with a deeply lined, bearded face and soft brown eyes — it seemed likely to me that this was my German carpenter, and perhaps that he was why I had been so unlucky in love all these years, for the immigrant had taken my imagination when I was just a girl.

Soon, however, the haze receded, and my eyes

cleared, and I gasped in recognition. It was Maxwell Hunter, and he laid his hand first on my forehead, then maternally touched my cheek. "She's not feverish," he said. His beard did not hide his wide smile.

"She's going to be all right, Mrs. Leahy," he said. Delicately physical, he steadied my wrist against his knee to take my pulse.

"Oh, but pale, pale, Dr. Hunter." Mother was repeating herself, a sure sign she was distressed.

"Isn't she very pale? You're pale, Reeni. Are you sure she's breathing, please? This has never happened before, Doctor. Is she breathing all right? Reeni? Reeni, speak to me!"

Normally my mother was a woman of few words, but her behavior this day was hysterical. She was twittering nonsense in a frail, high-pitched tone. I could almost see through the skin on her face; it was opaque and brittle like parchment, likely to shatter if she didn't stop talking so fast.

My own voice was buried so deeply in my throat that I could not speak. The healthy sheep were baaing in loud excitement and the sick ones, eyes wild and panicky, were snorting full kerchiefs of snot.

It was needle-nose Bess who roused me fully. While Dr. Maxwell Hunter and Mother stood discussing my health, Bess's pointed tongue probed my salty eyes and the nasty fluid in my mouth. She licked me fully awake, a duty she performed quickly so she could return to her own brood. I could hear them whimpering in the corner of the barn and resolved to find homes for all of her puppies.

By the time Mother and Dr. Hunter helped me into the house, it was dark. Despite his smiling demeanor, the episode had lasted long enough to concern the veterinarian, and he insisted on calling the town doctor. Doc Mason brought iron pills, declared me exhausted and prescribed bedrest.

Before I fell into a deep and satisfying sleep, I asked Mother about the sheep. "Did Dr. Hunter look at the lambs?"

"He did. It's a stubborn pneumonia and he's trying a new sulfa drug on them. He said he'll check on them tomorrow."

She studied me a moment, hovering like a hummingbird.

"He said he will call on you if you're up to it, but you don't look very well to me. I'll tell him not to bother you."

I tried to interrupt, remembering boys my mother had disallowed, men she'd sent away, but she was too quick. She turned out the light, disappearing behind the softly closed door.

FOUR DAYS AFTER I COLLAPSED IN THE barn, I was strong enough to pull on my boots and my shapeless, grain-dusty overalls. Uncle Alton had disposed of the dead lambs in a lime pit we kept beyond the fields, deep in the woods. He repaired the fence, released the sheep, and now we were cleaning the manure out of the barn. He filled the spreader pitchfork by pitchfork until the floor was clean and dry. Loads of heavy, sodden hay had already been spread on the fields, and the sickly aroma ravaged the fresh valley air. It was a pungent reminder of the year past and to some, the smell, though odoriferous, was a sign of passage.

I grabbed a fork and together my uncle and I worked in silence until the spreader was full.

"You want to unload her, Reeni?" He looked at me carefully, not at all sure I should be working so hard already.

Try as I might, I could never find any resemblance to my father in his brother. Where Father was tall and slender, Uncle Alton was stocky, a muscular short man; I was taller than my uncle. In fact, I didn't find a smidgen of family resemblance between the two of us, either.

But he did look out for me and now he said, "Never you mind, you stay off of that tractor. I'll take care of this load, then we're done."

While the sour smell of the rotting manure was not unpleasant, it did penetrate my air passages like a whiff of ammonia. The lambs, unaffected by the odor, zoomed mindlessly in and out of the barn to play their unique version of "king-of-the-hill." They had responded well to Dr. Hunter's new sulfa treatment. Altogether, only twelve died, instead of thirty, and the sick ones eventually recuperated and thrived.

The barn had also come alive. The annual chore of manure removal was almost done. That afternoon I would scrape and sweep the floor clean. The next few days, I would cheerfully spend with a bar of brown soap and bleach, enthusiastically washing down the walls of the pens, disinfecting the stalls.

Barn cleaning.

I had experienced desire before — rarely in relation to anyone specific, but now, half-embarrassed, half-elated, a longing to touch Maxwell colored each day. Whether I was doing chores or lying alone in my bed at the end of a busy day, an effervescence born of possibility bubbled within.

I DID NOT ACTUALLY SEE MAXWELL HUNTER again until October, when a colt rushed a barbed wire fence. But his smiling face, which had floated above me when I was on the floor of the barn, had begun to show up in my dreams. I was driven to see him again, and despite several neighborly, if uncharacteristic, calls to surrounding farms, I had been unable to arrange a coincidental encounter.

Even Mr. Delaney couldn't help me, and if there was anyone in town who could have given him a message, it was the old postmaster who was more gossipy than the church ladies and much less judgmental.

The post office was little more than a cabin with a

squeaky front door, and Mr. Delaney needed to take only three steps in any direction to move about. I found myself in town more often than ever before, searching for signs of the veterinarian. Finally, it was clear that I was not going to accidentally bump into the man the way I had during our very first encounter.

"Mr. Delaney," I said, painfully conscious that a woman of my age could easily slip into a swamp of towntalk, "Mr. Delaney, have you seen Dr. Hunter lately?" My casual tone was too obviously strained and the postmaster immediately caught on.

He tee-heed like a girl and told me he had not, that Dr. Hunter had been out of town for several weeks. "I believe he has family in Ithaca," he said, and tee-heed once more, causing me to resolve never to ask the fool a question about anything ever again.

Meanwhile, other less personal but permanent events were altering the countryside. Not only was I coddling my secret attraction, but that summer the Rural Electrification Act of 1935 finally, two years after it was passed, ushered electricity into our Donohue Flats. With a single flip of a switch, life in even the most rural corners of America was irretrievably transformed. There might have been huge European storm clouds certain to affect the climate in America, but for the time being, people in my world were involved in complicated, if ignorant, conversations about outlets and wiring, light bulbs and lampshades.

Dark corners of rooms were illuminated, and one bare light bulb cast the shadows of the sheep on the walls of the barn. Mother and I both were as excited as children at their first state fair when the old ice box made way for our first Kelvinator.

It was big. It was electric!

At the time, we were too preoccupied to care that Joey Baggs, the iceman, would need to find another job. The tools he used to cut the two foot blocks of ice would become expensive antiques, conversation pieces that today's young microwaving women hang in their kitchens.

For most of us, the coming of electricity was a grand march forward. But some country people distrusted the concept, and the accompanying monthly bill. They decided against using electricity then, and today, six decades later, there are still a few people in my unvarnished little corner of the world who refuse power.

Esther calls it plain crazy. "It's downright stupid in this day and age to be without electricity or indoor plumbing."

I shouldn't have gotten into it with her, but she should know that some people don't like the idea of utility companies poking around their yards, marching through the countryside, taking possession through what they call "eminent domain." They make an offer to buy an easement through your land, all right — for one dollar, and if you refuse to sell, they take you to court. You must give them power to give you power, and some people may resist that concept.

Others prize self-sufficiency; they're the ones who might still use horses to plow or refuse to use chemicals in their gardens. They try to live just like the old homesteaders did.

"Others," I hope I said pointedly enough, "can't afford to pay the bill."

I told Esther about Josephine Page who lives across the valley. From my place on clear mornings I can see the wood smoke billow from her chimney. She has no running water and says she doesn't need it.

"How can she possibly live like that," Esther sputtered. "Why should she? She's a crazy old recluse, that's why."

"She is not a recluse, and I don't know why you're so upset about it. What do you care? Why, Josey goes to church every week and shows her Holsteins at the county fair. I never heard of a recluse doing that."

I knew I had Esther there, and just for effect I told her that if I had it to do all over again, I wouldn't have water or electricity either.

"I can use an outhouse just fine. Used one all my life, and didn't need all of this light to read a book, either. That's what's wrong with today's youth. Television and record players."

Esther winced, but didn't reply. Placing a slice of bread in the toaster with a theatrical flourish, as if she herself had proved a point, she laughed and rolled her eyes. The girl does know how to get my goat.

The truth is the coming of electricity was a carnival, a fun arcade where every day new appliances showed up in the magazines, shiny symbols of modern luxury, toys for adults. I was as modern-thinking as anybody and paged through the Sears catalog, looking for the newest gadgets.

Radios were switched off and on like a teenager's mood, and surveys showed that people were listening nearly five hours a day. Hand irons, water pumps, washing machines, ranges, milking machines, electric motors, feed grinders, vacuum cleaners, electric chick brooders, all of these became possible with the electrical current provided by the REA.

Life became less isolated. I embraced the modern world, disregarding Mother's automatic misgivings, making no comment on the afternoon radio shows she tuned in every afternoon. The payment for this progress may have cost the young its youth, but I'm too old now to be concerned with consequences. There may be a sane undertone to those who refuse the niceties of electricity, plumbing, modern convenience foods, and fast cars, for these things reverberate with deterioration. I can see this now only because I am perched on the high wire of fate.

Chapter Nineteen

THE DAY CAME WHEN OUR OUTHOUSE, built long ago by my father, took an off-balance lurch to the left. I called on my Uncle Alton. His carpentry was not excellent, but better than his older brother's, and it was clear the time had come for our habits to change.

It was not an unusual structure, four feet by four feet with a sloped seven-to-five-foot roof. Maple boards with two seats, it was built smack in the middle of the back yard between the pond and the back porch, and over the years a wildly tangled single-petaled rose bush enveloped it in a baby-pig pink.

Wood is not an aggressive material but it has two elemental enemies: the more immediately devastating fire and the casually ruinous water. I'd neglected the roof of the construction for so long that rain had insidiously dripped onto the cherry sill beam, transforming its strength into a weak, sodden mass.

"Look, Uncle Alton, my finger goes right through it." The destroyed wood gave way as I poked my finger into its squishy surface. Beads of moisture squeezed out of the spongy material. The outhouse had seen its day.

"And anyway," I told him, "It's time this place gets some indoor plumbing."

"I'm surprised you're not tearing down the barn, too," Uncle Alton muttered. To him, the concept of elimination inside the house seemed raw and crude. He pulled at his mustache, deaf to anything else I had to say.

Taking his cue from my impatient uncle, his toothless sidekick Jeremy sneered, "Next you'll be bringing the pigs into the kitchen, Reeni."

But they dismantled the building, and a few weeks later, lead pipes ran spring water into the house, and I had a new bathroom with a toilet.

So many changes were occurring during that period that I really didn't begrudge the two men their complaints and resentment. The old, rural county roads in nearly all of New York State were being surfaced, made hard and unfamiliar. A fraternity of crabby old farmhands gathered on the porch of the general store just to watch the skittish horses go haywire when a Model-T clattered past. Somehow their laughter fueled resistance to the new ways, and Uncle Alton was one of the most boisterous members. But the noisy rejection of this gaggle of old men was futile, a death rattle.

I tried to be patient with him, but for reasons having to do with his liquor and an affection for cards, my uncle was never able to buy a farm of his own, nor find a woman to call his wife. My mother barely spoke to him, but I felt a warmth in the air when he walked into the room. After it became obvious that land was something he would never own, he took up the motto, "better to work for a farmer than be a farmer," claiming an informal stewardship of our homestead.

He and a disordered collection of his shabby friends kept my place in reasonable repair. In return, I saw to it that they ate one round meal a day. I also gave him a piece of property where he built a small house, and beyond the country music I sometimes heard, what went on in that handyman's mansion I would not want to hazard.

He guarded me, though, in an obliquely paternal way. Over the years I'd accidentally heard him mention my name, telling these men who so often shared his bottle, to stay away from my door.

"She's a bobcat," he told them, laughing. "Single life runs in the Leahy family for a reason." His was an odd method of protection I suppose, but it worked. It did keep men away.

While I felt a kinship with him, Mother could barely tolerate the man who was her husband's brother. He surely perturbed my mother more than anyone I've ever known. And he did it with the finesse of a Shakespearean actor, right up until his last mysterious day, which he spent in a motel in Miami.

According to Mother, too many Sundays had been

spoiled by "his heathen activities," and she hung up on his unusually peculiar call from Florida. It was his single trip outside of New York State, and all forty of his postcards postmarked from Pennsylvania to Florida are wrapped in tissue and packed upstairs in my biscuit tin of memories.

I don't know why he took such a trip; Florida seems like another country to me. But he did, and when finally he got to the end of the map he sent us a crate of moldy grapefruit, a jar of molasses which, after fifty years, is still in the pantry, and some kind of caramel pecan candy. That was very tasty, but so sweet! It stuck to my teeth and made them ache.

I'm convinced it's this Yankee weather that grows such rugged people. Those who survive a lifetime in the northeast develop a heartiness similar to that found in its wild animals. Those are wary creatures, all right, passing frigid winters here in the woods. Bobcats, coyotes, and deer. The occasional moose and ubiquitous bunny. Skunks and porcupines, chipmunks and coons. Red squirrels, gray squirrels, foxes and possum. They all remind me of Yankees.

The climate of the south does not accommodate a quick step. Its animals and people are unhurried. Uncle Alton told me they walk through a field like it's coated in blackstrap molasses, and their coon dogs and beagles, horses and cows, are covered with blood-sucking ticks and snakebites. Here in Carniff County, there are no poisonous snakes, or ticks, or poison ivy, and that one nasty spider, the recluse, lives up to his name hiding deep in woodpiles. Seldom is he sighted and I never knew anyone who was bitten. There's nothing too hazardous in these woods, except for the things we've brought in ourselves. Acid rain from the northern factories is killing some trees and illegal toxic waste dumping is not unusual. It's the people who soil their own nests; no animal alive does that.

The people from Maryland southward develop a sweet and sticky character. Where our maple syrup pours fast and light, their sorghum is thick and slow. Where northerners are brittle and icy, southerners are pliable and warm. A southern farmer has the time to get to know you. The ground isn't going to freeze overnight, and if you're able to chat with a southerner for twenty minutes straight, he'll never forget your name. A northerner never takes the time to know it in the first place.

Uncle Alton wrote that underneath it all, southerners still don't like us northerners very much. I can only conclude that most of our differences have something to do with Vitamin C, sugar, and weather.

I know none of the details, but in the end my uncle was shipped to Wichner by train and, after I filed all the proper papers, we buried him up on Leahy hill. It was just me, Mother, and the funeral director, and Mother refused to sing "Amazing Grace," so I sang alone.

I'm twitching like a fly-studded horse as I admit

this truth: my melodious voice that once could sing a sculpted soprano is now the cackle of an old hen. I did give Alton my best send-off, however. And while nobody even brought a casserole or sent a flower, a lacy sympathy card postmarked June 10, 1940 from Miami was sent by someone named Katerina. It smelled of perfume and vibrated with a story that I'll never know.

Uncle Alton and his scruffy crowd provided me with a clarified definition of possibility, or, more accurately, lack of possibility. While most successful men avoid sinful acts — excessive drinking, swearing, and especially gambling — Uncle Alton embraced them all. And while successful men make plans and keep pace with the times, my uncle skeptically withdrew. In matters of business, I imitated those serious farmers who prospered and sought ways to be modern. But secretly I wished like the devil that my eyes could sparkle like my Uncle Alton's when he was picking the banjo or two-stepping with a woman.

Chapter Twenty

THE SOUND OF FALLING RAIN CAN BE soothing in the middle of the night, like the song of tree swallows as they catch flies, skimming the surface of the pond like tiny shimmering dive bombers. Not that I can hear it anymore, but I can feel the vibrations of countless raindrops, pounding the roof in waves like soldiers attempting to take a hill. Too much rain in the daytime bleaches the colors of the season and soaks the spirit.

It's so dark today I need to strain my eyes to see this page. It just goes against my grain to turn on a light in the middle of the day. If I had the energy and it wasn't almost July, I would ask Esther to light a little fire. It wouldn't be the first time that summer flames have cracked in this fieldstone fireplace. Once it snowed two inches in July. All of my helpless young plants were killed. The cucumbers and squash died instantly and the peas and beans wore nasty black scars.

If *The Old Farmer's Almanac* is right, no color

will penetrate this dreary landscape for ten more days. Summer has been smothered like a brush fire, tortured into submission by clouds as gray as battleships and nearly as heavy. So, it seems, has Esther, whose featherweight footsteps nevertheless seem ponderous and unhappy.

Hay will mold in wet layers on the newly cut fields, vast puddles will suffocate even the most vigorous germinations, aborting growth, plundering the pantry. Onions will float on the surface of the shallow water, and the soaked soil will cling to dismayed, garden-gloved hands like chocolate pudding on a four-year-old's face. Those of us who need the normality of summer sunshine are losing patience. Too much weather can do that to a person; patience becomes as slippery as a muddy dirt road.

Patience. It's a virtue commonly confused with stubbornness, or worse, indifference. My own stubborn streak is as broad as my mother's was, but without it I could not have lived this long. Without it I would never have managed my romance with Dr. Hunter.

Though his face was clearly printed on every flat surface within my view, I did not see him for nearly two months after he treated the lambs.

I was afraid that Mother had somehow accomplished her goal, for no one was better able to communicate lack of enthusiasm than my mother, and whenever I mentioned his name, her face went rigid.

As Max later told me, she had telegraphed her displeasure to him which was, he said, why he didn't call on me sooner. He said he was hoping, just like I had been, to meet "serendipitously." It was a word that only an older man would use, when speaking about a romantic liaison, and his use of that word was perhaps why I fell in love with him.

Finally, though, on a cool dry October day, an emergency serious enough to call the veterinarian arose. A frisky new colt catapulted through the fence, and the rusty barbed wire slashed the chestnut as cleanly and deeply as a tiger's claws. Normally I would have mended the wounds myself, stitched the ripped coat closed, and pine-tarred the gashes. But my patience was exhausted; if I had to pay money to see this particular man, so be it. I led the terrified colt, blood dripping crosshatched patterns onto his butchered coat into his mother's stall, then ran like a schoolgirl to ring Dr. Hunter's office.

The lacerations were deep and lay like wide red ribbons across the colt's sweat-stained chest. Although I did have ulterior motives, I was honestly anxious that the wounds be tended quickly and Maxwell, sensing the urgency in my voice, promised to come immediately.

Suddenly aware of my blood-streaked barn coat and mannish, rubber barn boots, I rushed back to the house to change my clothes. Maxwell arrived so quickly that I was still applying a pink rouge to my startled cheeks when his Dodge, as shiny black as a polished piano, rolled into the driveway.

My mother was not the kind of ebullient woman who bounded out of the house to greet visitors, but as soon as his car ground to a stop, I heard a rush of rustling skirt and the squeaky screen door as it slammed shut. From my bedroom window, I saw her standing stiffly next to Maxwell's car, head cocked up at him like a robin listening to the ground for the movement of a worm. I recognized the interception. I didn't bother to wash my hands, and hurried down the stairs.

Maxwell was getting back into his car as I bolted out of the house. "I described the injuries to the good doctor and he agrees you can repair them yourself, dear," Mother said, turning to look directly at me. Tension surged between us until I marched past her and extended my hand to the doctor.

"Maybe I'll just take a look anyway, Mrs. Leahy," Maxwell said, and we walked to the barn together as if we had been walking next to each other all of our lives.

For a while I was furious with my mother for her interference, but surely it was a simple matter of fear that motivated her. I should have told her that if Maxwell Hunter wanted me — if anyone had ever wanted me — he would get both of us. But Mother never quite believed that she could not be erased.

HE SAID I SHOULD HAVE BEEN NAMED PA-
tience, but what Maxwell considered an opales-
cent virtue others have more correctly recognized as
a frank and marble-glazed obstinance.

"I'm sure my mother would disagree with you
about that, Dr. Hunter," I replied. "Patience is not
even my middle name."

He smiled at me as I held the renegade colt still,
rubbing away his wild-eyed frenzy. The air in the
barn was not dusty but clear, as if vacuumed by
a diligent maid. Sunlight slipped through cracks in
the walls, poured through the open windows, which
framed a few grazing sheep. Off and on a ewe flicked
an ear, which floated like a small pink sail on a sea
of green. Motionless, she lifted her head, body muscles adjusted for flight, listening to us, then relaxed,
burying her nose deep again into the knee-deep
grass.

"Ah, but look at you right now," Maxwell said
quietly, as he tacked each stitch, slowly closing the
wounds with thick cotton thread. "Some would try
to rush me, try to hurry this job. But not you, Miss
Irene. You need to have patience to be good with
animals and you're as good as I've seen. You handle your sheep like a teacher handles first graders. I
think you could get the wildest animals to feed from
your hand."

Briefly, he looked into my eyes and a warm flush
escaped from my collar, traveling north over my
face in an eternally hot wave. His words wrapped

around me like a long wool coat, and my breath left. I had no response, could think of nothing to say. Instead I held the colt's head tighter, absently watching the iridescent blue wings of three tree swallows rise and dip over the pond. I did not want this man whose black hair was salted with time, whose face was a map of kind lines, who looked at me as if he knew my midnight secrets, to call me "Miss" Irene.

Soon the graceful swallows would fly south along with the Canada geese, the red-winged blackbirds, the robins and nearly all of the other birds except the sparrows, jays and chickadees. But for now the tree swallows were content to buffet the black glassy water, striking surface insects from the sky the way the fish strike them from below. The rings they caused to lap softly at the edge of the shore were exactly the same, and suddenly the band of similarity between the two creatures doubled in width.

As I stared across the pond, an image of my father and me slowly emerged. We were walking up the Pike Road to go turkey hunting. I was holding his hand. It was strong and capable; my fingers couldn't wrap all the way around his.

"You have grace in the woods, Reeni," he had whispered. *"Birds land right on your hand."*

Max glanced at me quickly. "Tilt his head a bit to the left," he said. "Are you all right?"

"Yes, of course. I was just thinking about my father. You remind me of him a little."

157

I concentrated on his steady hands. He was intent on his work and did not notice my own trembling. The leaves swirled around our knees, fluttering in the air like moths as he completed the last stitch. I did not want him to finish. It would mean that he would have to leave again and this flowering of emotion was too fresh to cut.

When he was satisfied that the wounds were well sewn, we led the colt into his mother's stall. The two animals vibrated, a reciprocally nervous pair, assaulted yet again by these two-legged creatures with round holes in their faces from which came loud and impolite commands. The colt was a beauty, not a workhorse but an Arabian cross. I'd accepted the mare as a trade for some sheep; that she was bred was an unexpected added attraction. The mare's elegant conformation enticed me at once, but Mother was unimpressed.

"Those were registered ewes, Reeni. You should have taken money for them. A riding horse is the most inefficient animal on a farm. You know that. Useless they are, high strung and finicky. Get yourself a good pair of pulling ponies if you must have horses. At least they have a purpose."

I knew she was right, but sometimes a person's decisions are not based on common sense. "I'm keeping these horses, Mother, if only as pasture ornaments. The flock needed to be culled, anyway. Two hundred ewes are enough."

She snorted like a horse herself, her face fleshily

contorted in derision. Gypsy and Pat galloped across the field of my mind; I knew Mother was thinking about them, too.

Everything else lost significance as Maxwell and I stood close to each other outside of the stall. The mare was distressed and skittish. We waited quietly while she nuzzled her foal. Afraid to look at Maxwell, I stared at the animals, holding the doctor's presence aloft like a glass of fine wine. Finally the colt calmed, and sunk his soft muzzle deep into his mother's inflated teats. She answered, gently nudging, swishing her long and graceful auburn tail, snapping away flies and making half-moon patterns in the dirt.

"I haven't named him yet," I whispered, loathe to disturb our tranquillity. Maxwell turned toward me and for the first time I looked into his eyes.

"I'll call you Reeni," he said, "if you call him Patience." He leaned down and put his lips on mine.

He smelled like the woods, like oak leaves and moss, and he was broad and strong like my father. I was afraid my mouth was taut and repellent on his. I was afraid my hair was too short and my expression too apprehensive. I was afraid that he would recoil, and that my body, rigid as a concrete statue in his arms, would proclaim its circumstantial chastity.

I hid my face, its clownish cosmetics so inexpertly applied, in the tweedy wool of his chest. I was a dry, foolish spinster who had somehow, after years of seclusion, sunk like a stone into this strange quagmire, and when the split second was presented, when Maxwell took my chin in his bear paw and looked quizzically into my eyes, I could have taken one step back. Instead I leaned into him, put my arms around his neck, and fell in.

Perhaps it was my own maturity which liberated my body at that particular time, for thirty-seven is a nondescript year in a life. Yet it is a year that hints of adjournment. Perhaps I finally kicked away the stumbling blocks Mother continuously threw across my path, for why should she captain my body when I was lucky enough to meet a man who loved my flaws and my season?

It was not until the next spring, after a winter of Friday night suppers with my grim, suspicious mother, that we began to see each other more than once a week, for the drive from Max's home in Ithaca was long and the snow-covered roads perilous.

"Soon, Reeni," he told me, "Soon I will sell the house and move my practice closer to Donohue Flats."

Spring is a farm vet's busiest time: All the cows in the county suddenly seem to demand attention. Max's growing practice devoured days at a time, and I was pleased when he said, "Sundays are ours, Reeni. We'll spend the whole day together from now on."

Mother complained bitterly that I had lost interest in the farm. She remained as icy as a mountain top around Max, and his patient attempts to defrost her were in vain.

"Where is he from, Reeni?" Mother questioned me.

"Ithaca."

"He was born in Ithaca? No one was born in Ithaca, everyone there comes from somewhere else."

"Mother," I would reply, exasperated. "I suppose you want to know his date of birth and social security number, too."

It was nearly eight months after he treated the chestnut colt that we motored to Howe Caverns. By then, Max had become an untrained vine, a morning glory coiled in a very personal way around my compliant, pale-skinned body. He was fluid and kind, massaging my stiff neck and tense shoulders.

The blanket we laid on the floor of the woods or in an open field or along a sandy creek or, once, on a drizzly day, in the back seat of his Dodge, matched the color of the burgeoning green meadows. The first few times I lay on it like brittle blown glass, but Max enchanted me and I came to believe that I was not dry and finished, but blooming radiantly, like a white, plump-hipped rose in the sun.

Sometimes we went to the matinee at the Wichner Cinema, or I packed a lunch and we took long, luxuriously impure drives in the country. When we had to be apart, I'm afraid I was daisy-headed and unfocused. He split my life in two parts, and even now I sometimes reconstruct my thoughts in terms of before and after Dr. Maxwell Hunter.

The day we were going to Howe Caverns, Max used

all of his charm to win one smile from my mother. "I studied at the Cornell Vet School and I don't believe Ithaca, with all of its streams and gorges, can compare to Howe Caverns, Mrs. Leahy," he said. "Maybe you have some caves on your property."

The corner of her lips barely rose; Max had won a victory and his grin was infectious.

"Well, all I know about Howe Caverns is that Mr. Howe discovered them in 1842, three years before this house you're standing in was built. Reeni's father always meant to take me there."

"Why don't you come with us, Mrs. Leahy?" Max said enthusiastically. He'd hooked and almost landed her, and while Mother self-consciously picked at the hem of her apron, Max placed his arm around my waist and beamed. Then she flatly refused. But after a winter of her blatant disapproval, headway was being made.

In the end there were two reasons I was glad she didn't come with us, one selfish, one not. It was a damp chilly place, a place where you traded color and light and the atmosphere of the living for the dank artificial air of a crypt. Mother would not have liked it at all.

It's been said that the part of a cave touched by a human hand dies like a leaf in a fire. While Max eagerly roamed the belly of the vast hole, feeling the dark intricacies of the walls, I kept my arms folded tightly against my chest, expecting bats.

"It's the symmetry of nature that's so astounding,

Reeni," he said. "See how the stalagmites form up from the floor to meet the stalactites that grow down from the ceiling?"

I agreed that symmetry is marvelously apparent in nature, but the cave made me claustrophobic and I hoped no one discovered anything like it on my land.

Later, I described the place to Mother. "It feels like somewhere you go to die. The dripping darkness — it's too spooky, too far under the ground for me. I couldn't breathe."

"You're such a fuss budget, Irene, always upset about something. And why must you wear pants on Sunday, for heaven's sake?"

She fretted while I fumbled with my hat and jacket. Maxwell seemed completely indifferent to my wardrobe and — this may sound strange — he loved to scratch my close-cropped hair, as if I were a poodle. The women in the magazines, with their hourglass silhouettes and padded shoulders were much too squeezed in for me. If pants were good enough for Hepburn, they were good enough for anyone.

Talk of my wardrobe was trivial, considering what I had to tell Mother, but her fussy mood strangled my bittersweet one. The most important news of my life was left in the closet, a small velvet box hidden in the pocket of my black cloth coat.

"I should have gone with you and your smart Dr. Hunter, but he didn't really want me along. All my life I've heard about Howe Caverns, but your father never took me to see them."

"Why not?" I asked with little interest. Since she wouldn't acknowledge Max's courtesy, I didn't feel very mannerly myself. From the moment he entered my life, disapproval had resonated habitually in her tone of voice, and today I needed to avoid yet another circular argument. Her eyes darted about the kitchen like a housefly that senses the swatter and refuses to land.

"Why not?" I repeated, glancing in her direction as I removed the pins from my hat. There was much on my mind.

"If you want me to talk to you at all, you should at least pretend to listen." She watched me from across the room for a long time to be certain she had my attention, then quietly continued.

"The cavern is in Cobleskill, over two hours from here by car, Irene. We never even had a car, you know that. You didn't see us travel like that. We went to town functions. Grange dinners. Memorial Day cake walks. Fourth of July parades."

She paused, staring at the floor.

If it hadn't been for Maxwell, I would have been just like her, never seen Howe Caverns or Katharine Hepburn picture shows. I waited attentively; the conductor's baton had been tapped and after a long, riveting silence, she completed her thought. "Once in a while I even got your father to go to church."

This last was meant to provoke me since the only time I myself stepped into the tiny Methodist church was for the occasional wedding or more frequent funeral. But like clockwork, Evie Dalton drove around the driveway to the back porch every Sunday morning at ten after nine to take Mother to services. They wore their plain, black Sunday bonnets fifty-one weeks of the year. Easter Sunday they were discarded like old fruit, and in the spirit of renewal, fanciful ones perched high on their proud topknots. Mother's one fearless concession to style was the embroidered lace handkerchief that she pinned like a piece of jewelry on the lapel of her drab coat. I had learned to get down to the barn early on Sunday mornings, for the way she fussed and fluttered about the house, as she dressed for church, irritated me more than sand in my salad.

"Mother," I sighed, unwilling to argue about my irreligious ways. But she shook her head as if freeing it from cobwebs.

"You know what I should have done, Reeni. You know what I really should have done?"

Now I was the one who shook my head.

"I should have had someone take me to Wichner. I should have gotten on the train, and I should have gone to Howe Caverns by myself." She lowered her head and turned away.

A WEEK HAD PASSED SINCE MAX HAD PROposed, and by then the romance, the aroma of him and the day, the background loveliness that would have bubbled forth in the telling, had become too intimate to share.

On the way back from Howe Caverns, he stopped at a pretty spot along the Carniff River. Max's shiny car glinted in the sun, blackly reflecting the sky and trees. We spread a red and white tablecloth next to it on the ground, and while I unpacked fried chicken and biscuits, fresh strawberries and chocolate cake, he leaned against the fender of his Dodge, watching me. He held a small black box in the palm of his hand, which he lightly drummed with two fingers.

I laughed. It was good to be on top of the ground instead of under it. The tableau was like a scene from one of the picture shows, and I was glad my mother had stayed home. Max would surely not have chosen this moment to propose if she had been with us. My instincts went raw with expectation.

"Why are you tapping that box, Max? What do you have there?"

Casually he tossed it onto the red and white table-cloth.

"Open it." It was a declarative sentence, but his tone dropped a question mark at the end, and his confident smile had straightened to a thin-lipped stripe.

The diamond in the ring absorbed all sights and sounds. It was small, but burned in my eyes like a spark in the dark. It showcased my snakeskin hands. The ragged nails and dirt-stained knuckles had never before embarrassed me. Flustered, I dropped it in the grass, just as Maxwell Hunter asked me to marry him.

He went down on his knee to pick up the ring and finished the proposal. "Will you marry me, Reeni, when I get home from Europe?"

And with those words World War II exploded like a grenade in my own backyard.

Chapter Twenty-One

THE RAIN HAS WASHED AWAY THE PLEAS-
ures of this month, even the intrepid spring flowers
are flat on the ground, and my house has become a
dripping cave. Water collects in gallon coffee cans on
the stairs.

I should tend to these insidious leaks. They'll soak
the wooden cells, transforming the timber into sour
mash, just like the old outhouse. There was a time
the sight of one feeble drip would have launched me
into instant repair, but not now. I'll just have Esther
empty the cans as many times as she must before the
drying sun returns. I can wait out the longest rain.

Still, this rancorous storm, dramatic, restless and
stubborn, is beginning to test me. Relentlessly, it
slaps the side of the house like wet rubber sheets. The
unprotected trees writhe in the wind and threaten to
snap. Their leaves sag low, dripping water that has
become acidic and unhealthy.

An unpleasant moldy odor has moved into the
house, occupying all that is soft and pliable. It clings

like bad breath to my hair and skin. The dampness invades my bones and most of the day I stay in bed, shoulders wrapped tightly in my brown crocheted afghan. It too smells like wet, rotting leaves.

When I do rise, it's in stages, unfolding in segments like a wooden ruler. Once as sturdy as a pair of stilts, these reticent legs are now no stronger than sawdust. I lift them first, forcing my arms to move them one by one until they dangle like willow branches over the side of the bed. Then I shift my weight to the ugly metal walker. It's a tangle of a body that houses my soul, as rusty and knotted as the barbed wire that lacerated the little chestnut colt. That colt was born under a dark star; not two years later lightning struck him dead. My lifeline, like his, is tattered.

Esther brought me the walker from the Social Services. It's a handy enough thing, but why don't they come in colors, painted paisley, perhaps, or a nice cheerful blue. It punches my pass to the world of invalids. I did find one good use for it. Esther was furious with me, but I couldn't have climbed the stairs without that walker.

DEVOTING SO MUCH THOUGHT TO MAXwell Hunter spurred this nostalgic old mule up those narrow stairs. It was the photographs —they finally pulled me out of my bed, calling and calling, summoning me up into that attic like a bird dog to water.

I was as fluttery as a sparrow as I pushed through the dusty puffs of dresses that hung in hot space, victims of fashion or passionless dry rot. Rodent signs appeared here and there — a nibbled floorboard, seeds or scat, and musty books spilled out of cardboard boxes. My flashlight was dimming, but I knew just where to look; the box hadn't been touched for fifty years.

Soon I was back in the daylight, sitting on a steamer trunk with the prize in my lap. I looked at the familiar flock of sheep etched on its tin lid. Lying peacefully under a maple tree, they looked like so many of the photographs I've taken here on the farm. Nabisco must have been a very good company to place such a pretty picture on a biscuit tin.

Everything was there as I'd remembered — the ring, nested in its velvet box, the Howe Caverns ticket stub, the moth-eaten turkey feather, and the faded tintype of Billy and me. Uncle Alton's yellowed postcards from his trip south were there, and tucked under it all was the short stack of letters from Max. I untied the musty pale blue ribbon and coughed.

My dearest Irene,

This is just a short note to make me feel in touch with you. It's been only a day and already I miss you like the sky misses the stars. But I will not dwell on our separation, for this is just the beginning of a long journey. I will come home to you and we will marry. We will build the flock and breed race horses. Why not? Your mother will get used to the idea, rest assured! How I love you, my precious Reeni. Remember to give Patience an apple for me.

All my love,
Max.

We wrote letters for a year. The last one, postmarked from Tunisia, is the most thumbprinted and fragile:

Dearest Irene:

In this place I am the officer in charge of body parts. Veterinarians know more about flesh and blood than some others and my job is to match and identify, sending the proper pieces home in the proper pine box. The human doctors are kept too busy for this gruesome task. It is hopeless, full of misery. The carnage is horrendous, Reeni. Please God let it be over soon. I write to you in bloodstained clothes, stinking like a dead animal and still I believe in our future. I tell you these things not to upset you, dearest Reeni, but to communicate how hopeful and joyous our future will be. No matter what occurs to me here, I will always love you. I was so happy to get the pictures. The farm is beautiful and "Mom" looks well. But you, my love, you are the first face I see every morning. I kiss your photo and keep it with me close to my heart. Don't forget me, Reeni and please, be patient.

Love,
Max

Two months after I received his last letter, a small pastel pink envelope with no return address appeared in the mailbox.

Dear Miss Irene Leahy:

This is just a short note to give you the terrible news about my father. There is no kind way to tell you. The death notice Mom received from the Army is enclosed. He told me about you, but I'm not sure you knew that he had a nineteen-year-old daughter. I'm a student in Romance Languages at Cornell. Pop visited me every Saturday afternoon. My mother and father had not lived together for five years but nothing was legal. I'm afraid he was worried that the truth would upset your plans to marry. He did, I'm sure, fully intend to obtain a legal separation and divorce. He simply ran out of time. I'm terribly sorry, but I felt someone should contact you.

Very truly yours,
Melissa A. Hunter

I continue to wonder when, and how, he intended to tell me. Betrayal and the loss of a child are the only things that will soak a woman's pillow like mine was that night.

"I never did trust the man," Mother said, rubbing my back until dawn.

I KNEW IT WOULD UPSET ESTHER THAT I went to the attic by myself. Her face, pinched as a clothespin, seemed to fold back on itself, and it took all day for the lines to fall back in place. I don't care; I nearly always do exactly as she says, and if she wants to slam the door when she leaves, that's all right with me.

I must admit it was a little lucky that she showed up in time to help me back down those narrow stairs. As she told me three or four times, I could have fallen and broken my hip. But I needed to take the chance, and with the walker I had six legs, plenty to climb a few old steps. Knocking over the coffee cans of water made a mess, but that's not what made Esther so mad.

"Irene Leahy," she said, mopping the puddles dry, "Don't you ever give me a scare like that again."

She didn't give me the chance to explain, and just as I was about to hand her the black velvet box, she slipped on a wet spot on the floor. It wasn't a bad twist, but I watched as her face flushed a fire engine red, and her temper stirred in a way that warned me to say no more.

I listened quietly as she rubbed her ankle and

railed. "This could have happened to you," she said, practically panting. "Look at poor Joe," she said, pointing to the trembling dog, "Look how upset he is."

Finally she left me alone, and I took the ring from my nightgown pocket. It's a sweet little diamond, and I want her to have it.

Chapter Twenty-Two

I HAD NO IDEA WHEN I GOT MY FIRST CAM-
era that such a simple device would solidify my
memories, provide a past to hold in my hand. It was
Mother's idea to buy it, and thanks to her my image
of Maxwell Hunter is still sharp, as is the pain.

The day I bought the camera, I was peeling tomatoes, dropping the Big Girls with their blushing
fat cheeks into the hot water just long enough for
their skins to slip off their faces, when Mother rushed
into the kitchen. Dust followed Mr. Cody's Hudson
past the mailbox and all the way up Pike Road. We
were the last mailbox on his route and like a bored
trailhorse, the mailman's attention was focused on
speeding home.

Waving a handful of letters, Mother said, "Look
at this, Reeni. Kodak has those square little box
cameras on sale."

A talent for drawing never presented itself to
me — Father was the artist in my family — but taking snapshots required no skill. There was extra egg

and wool money in the tin can on my desk; we dropped coins into it like a wishing well. So I sent off for the camera. Soon I had a hobby.

Initially, I started taking pictures of the garden just for practice. Not until my mother died did the vegetable garden become my own personal friend; my companion for the summer, for Mother did not share her garden's joys. She tended it like a sentinel; my role was to plow the dirt and till and weed, but not, while my mother was alive, was I to direct its motion, plan its rotations, sow its seed. Mother controlled the garden, turning it over to me only after her lifeless body was buried up on Leahy Hill. Even then, it seems to me, she judged the roundness of my tomatoes and the size of the snap bean harvest.

In the beginning I took many pictures of my mother, but soon she discovered that she despised seeing photographs of herself and she began to avoid the camera the way an irritable cat avoids affection. The moment she spotted me with it she scowled, dipped her head and turned her back. But there is one snapshot of her without an aura of invasion. Stooped over a sea of knee-high tomato plants, a straw hat shades her face, but that day she glanced up from the weeding just long enough for my camera to document in her lined face a woman at home in her garden. I had captured the face under the mask, the same face I remembered as a child as she watched the lambs from the parlor window.

My box of photographs are faded now, mere out-
lines of the original image. I brought them downstairs with me, perhaps to share with Esther. They
give me pleasure. I examine the yellow-edged
squares of paper like a mother who searches the face
of her adult child. If the removed and preoccupied
body is no longer pertinent to her own, it is, in some
physical way, related and for that reason, fascinating
to her and to her alone.

A WELL-TENDED PLOT OF LAND DEVELOPS
an inner rhythm and balance of its own. It develops a personality. Sometimes, annoyed at the
weather, marauding chickens, or abusive gardening,
it can become obstinate ground. As if an ill-natured
bird had dropped a poisonous seed in the middle of
the asparagus, the garden will refuse to give up its
progeny. The soil rebels.

It saddens me that quack grass and burdocks are
digging deep into the garden where my mother and
I spent so many hours of our lives. The enemy weeds
drink nutrients, kill fertility, and all I can do is witness the ruin. The garden went before me, but not
before my mother, who would have died without it.

Even before the first stroke, which slapped her
face hard and without mercy, Mother's joints were as
swollen and motionless as the hard twisted knuckles
of an ironwood tree. Her voice had turned high, the
pitch of a wet, muddy boot sliding across a newly

waxed floor. In the winter she rarely left the house; the weather demanded too much of her bones. But in summer, when the sun was hot and soothing, she perched on the back porch rocker, watching me work in the garden, vociferously conducting its growth.

I was not fond of her critical review of my planting, and there was one day when the sun's heat blended with the sound of her demanding voice in such a way that I felt leaden, burdened with the planting chores.

"Not so close, Reeni. You'll crowd the peas." She pounded her cane on the porch rail to get my attention. "If you're going to plant a garden do it right from the start." She jabbed the baton crisply, like Toscanini, pointing and waving. "I don't think the beds are well enough prepared."

"Yes, they are, Mother, and I am *not* crowding the peas." Settling down into her rocker, she watched intently as I buried the onion sets just so, deeply and with ample space between, or planted the peas one hard green heart by one. She created a fast-paced tempo, but in this climate plants do need a proper start. There isn't much time to live.

"Well," she huffily maintained, "there's little point in careless gardening. There's a season of work in front of you, Irene, and you may as well make it as easy on yourself as possible."

That night sleep was a slippery fiend. It was 1965 and the United States had been continuously bombing North Vietnam since March. Pictures of babies, their skin split and smoking like grilled meat,

kept me awake. Fifteen Donohue Flats boys had
been drafted. Visions of Maxwell Hunter and his
vivid descriptions of the war that claimed his life
floated above me. I tossed covers off and on. The
memory of his betrayal, of his wartime death, of my
brusque impatience with all the men I encountered
after Maxwell, mingled with the images of wartorn
jungles and the peaceful beauty of the garden outside.

A deep and exhausted sleep as welcome as a sea-
side vacation finally wrapped me in darkness, and I
disregarded the soft bumping noise on the other side
of my bedroom wall. I did not hear Red when she
pushed past my bedroom door. It was a region she
herself declared unfit, and the dog never came into
my room. She favored my mother whose job did not
require her drowning cross-bred puppies or stitching
wounds. Red was a sensitive dog and could never
forgive me for such acts.

But this singular summer night was like none other
and Red put aside her rage. Ignoring her own rules,
she whimpered loudly and jumped on my bed. Her
nails dug into my chest as she frantically licked my
mouth and eyes. She excavated my face with her
hot collie nose until I struggled out of a blue watery
dream. Whining, she scratched red, painful lines in
my skin until I heard the sickening thuds on the other
side of my bedroom wall. Finally, I was as alert as
the dog.

You might expect a frail eighty-three-year-old

woman to perform her last act with grace and elegance: to dance with mortality like a lady. Maintenance of decorum, however, is a notion conceived for the self-conscious.

My mother was a stubborn conquest, her heart ground to a slow stop, but life poured from her body like water from a hose. It rushed out of every flailing extremity, contorting her body, cracking her brittle skull on the wall until the lathe and plaster splintered and a slippery sham of blood covered her face. She sputtered, outraged at such indignity. In a final gasp for another violent breath, she clawed her fingertips to slivers on the wide pine floorboards.

Mother's cruel death, a grim contrast to my indistinct concept of dying peacefully in sleep, skirted the comfort of insensibility, denied my mother the anesthesia of unconsciousness. Her life escaped in panting terror while I tried to contain her flailing body, folding it in my arms like a broken fan.

We huddled on the floor, rocking to the tick of the clock that squatted like a bomb on her tidy bureau. We did this until the roosters called to each other and dawn reflected blood red in the mirror. We did this until Mother was as still as a block of ice in the dead of winter and her lips were as colorless as a January morning.

She rectified no lies and whispered only one sentence before she died. "You should have married,

Irene," was what she said, then gurgled and was gone.

I unlocked my aching joints and gathered wash cloths and water and her favorite lavender cologne. I changed her stained nightgown and sponged her naked body. Cleaned and pretty in a frilled nightgown, I placed her in the bed like a sparrow in a shoebox. I scrubbed the bloodied walls and floor, then inspected myself for damage, for I was sixty-five, almost elderly, and collecting government money for the first time in my life.

My mother's salvation through which she worshipped her God were her sheep. And while most of my own life I buried the subject of salvation in a hole behind more immediate mental chores, a dense jungle of intricate greenery has grown from it now. The symmetry of sheep grazing in the lush fields, of healthy twins born in sub-zero temperatures, of stew simmering on the stove in winter, of dogs diving into the pond, and cats stretching in the sun, there is enough in all of that to satisfy my spiritual needs.

Still, for my mother I knelt at the deathbed and whispered the Lord's Prayer, because I felt I should. It was also the only one I knew well enough to recite out loud.

Downstairs, Red was nervously scratching at the door to go outside. I opened the creaky screen door and she ran all the way across Pike Road. Suddenly, she stopped at the foot of the trees in a clearing lit by the early morning sun. Ears up and eyes shining like polished mahogany, she tucked her left leg back under her chest and lay down in one graceful motion. We stared at each other for a long time, her with a wild intensity of purpose and me with the knowledge that this was a dog on her way.

If she had a hat she would have tipped it as she gracefully unfolded her slender legs and turned to lope over the hill. A flash of red rust against the forest, I expected never to see her again, but a few days later, when we buried my mother on a sunny, calm June day not unlike today, I saw her standing perfectly still on the barn bridge, watching us. For weeks thereafter she penetrated my shallow sleep at midnight, howling in the forlorn way only those deep in mourning can bear. When finally she stopped, I remember dreaming that Red had found a happier farm, one with sheep and some children.

I HAD TO GET PERMISSION FROM THE county to bury my mother, even though it was on her own property, and state regulation required that the emergency squad transport her body to Booker's Funeral Parlor in Wichner where I was required to sit with her body for three days before I could finally put her to rest. I paid John Booker five hundred and eighty-nine dollars for a shiny coffin that was not pine, not crafted by a neighbor's kind hand. Eighty-three bells did not toll.

People sent sympathy cards, but not many came

to the house, for nearly everyone Mother knew was too ill, too ornery, or dead. Those few who brought dishes of food seemed embarrassed. They were anxious to leave and comfortless. In less than a half century since Father died, simple things had become complicated, complicated things unmanageable.

I always saw to it that the graves were tended, and it pains me now that they are not. Billy's concrete marker is slightly askew, as if the breeze that seems to live there in the family plot is wearing it away. The forsythias I planted so many years ago still cascade brightly golden at the head of each tombstone, but the tiger lilies have overtaken the rosebushes and no one trims the grass like I did, with sheep shears and scythe. Only in winter before the snow buries the stones does the place look drearily neat.

Maybe — since he was the one who offered — I will allow Reverend Thorne to cut the overgrowth, tidy up the graves. After all, I should get something in return for all of his talk about Pine Manor, and he could use some sun. Besides, he does have that Maxwell Hunter smile.

Chapter Twenty-Three

THE BODY SHEDS ITS STRENGTH LIKE A snake its skin. I've seen it happen both to animals and to people. Energy dissipates and vigor disappears. It's no surprise that deterioration kills an appetite. Yesterday, Esther said she's going to have to start feeding me if I continue to refuse to eat, that I'm getting too lazy.

"And you need more exercise, too, Miss Irene. Your muscles will turn to spaghetti." She placed a plate of food on the table in front of me.

"That looks more like finger paint than food," I told her, "And when eating becomes exercise, you can just put me out of my misery, please. This stuff you're giving me is soft as potter's clay and tastes like it, too. It makes eating a nauseous act."

Fact is, she's the one who's failing to thrive. She's losing meat faster than I am. Bones are jutting out of her cheeks and face powder cannot conceal those raccoon rings under her eyes. Still, she persists in pestering me. This morning she said, "Two of my other clients are moving to Pine Manor Home, Miss Irene. They've been on the waiting list for over a year."

What could I say to that? Except for The Last Exit — a floor at Carniff General inhabited by the poor and walking dead — Pine Manor is the only nursing home in Wichner. Pets are not allowed. Cards and bingo are.

"I brought you some information about it." She ducked her head to one side as she handed me the flyer.

Puppies do that if they've been beaten, and I recognized the motion. Mother was the only person I knew who could make me feel endangered that same way, especially if I tried to tell her something she did not want to hear. So I took a deep breath and politely accepted the slick brochure.

I scanned it, quickly reviewing the photographs. One was of some Brillo-haired ladies about twenty years younger than I am, sitting at a round table in a dining hall. They were eating out of Styrofoam plates with plastic spoons. That ruined my appetite, I must say. I gave Joe a pat and slipped the advertisement under the bed.

"Doesn't look like such a bad place, really," I told Esther.

And except for the wheelchairs and the empty eyes floating like fish in a sea of loose skin, it really doesn't.

OF COURSE, PINE MANOR PROBABLY ISN'T AS damp as this old farmhouse. The rain has stopped, but the sun is bashful, and I fear this summer is passing abnormally. The evil lightning that slashed across the sky like a whitehot whip has softened into sporadic illuminations of the valley, and thunder now rumbles gently in the distance, brutalizing some other town. Joe remains skittish, though. He still gets as jittery as a cricket when he sees a flash of lightning, and claws his way under the old kitchen stove.

If the barn is the heart of a farm, the kitchen is its heartbeat. Every smart dog knows that the barn may be more fun, but a rug on the kitchen floor is paradise. In our house, there was always a dog under the scarred kitchen table, with its one crippled leg and six durable, t-back chairs. Around that table is where vitality was renewed, farm plans drawn, goals evaluated, and bodies warmed and nourished.

I wonder if the ladies at Pine Manor miss their own kitchens, their refrigerators and stoves and kitchen utensils? Anyone who has cooked a lifetime has a favorite frying pan or stockpot, a measuring cup or spoon. Kitchens promise such pleasure; there is nothing more agreeable after a bone-tiring day of farm work than the aroma of a bubbly stew and a batch of cooling biscuits. The Pine Manor farm wives have forfeited their kitchens. Surely they are not happy about that.

The walls of my kitchen were last papered in 1958.

The rug beaters had been put away, the ammonia-bathed windows were as clear as the air, and Mother's knees and mine were finished with spring cleaning for another year. Mother removed her kerchief and stepped back to review the newly scrubbed walls of the kitchen. "They still look dirty, Reeni," she said.

Well, my hands were chapped and my back was aching after scouring the whole room from top to bottom, but I could see that though the walls were clean, they did look dull. I went to my desk and dipped into the cash tin.

"There might be enough here to buy some wallpaper, you know," I said, stacking the coins into several dollars. That afternoon we piled into my '56 Chevy for a jaunt to Wichner in search of the perfect pattern. At first we were like eager brides, poring over the thick book of samples, but it soon became apparent that we had different approaches to the intricate science of decoration.

"You don't want that dark green, Reeni. The flowers are too big and wrong for a kitchen. Remember, we're going to have to live with this for a few years. You want to make the right choice. I'm partial to this one," she said, pointing out a red and white check that looked too much like a board game for me.

Each turn of the book page generated a rain of words. Until then I had not recognized my mother's interest in interior decoration. Amused, I sat back on the stool and pointed to another choice.

"What do you think about this one?"

It was a nice design, I thought — red clocks and coffee pots sprinkled across a background of small sunny yellow polka dots. But after a full afternoon of searching, Mother's vote remained firm for the red and white check.

"It's bold and makes a statement," she said, surprising me.

"What's it saying," I asked. "Bring out the checkers?"

With that, Mother opened her purse, pulling out a page torn from the *Ladies Home Journal.* There, big as life in an article entitled "The Modern Kitchen of the Fifties" was a picture of a kitchen all done up in the same red and white wallpaper. "It's bold and it makes a statement," the caption read.

"Your father would have liked it," she said smugly, sealing the decision.

Now the paper is peeling and streaked, darkened with grease and years, but the longer I live with it, the more I like it. That's why I never re-papered the walls, because altering something as permanent as a wall might change my memories, erase a part of my life. One finds one cannot take chances.

It was in the kitchen that the day's activities were reviewed, *The Evening Star* read, our wet socks hung from the stove to dry. It was in the kitchen, half asleep from the exhaustion of lambing, that Mother and I took turns leaning against the sink, floating slippery, newborn, hypothermic lambs in a tub of warm water for hours, hours that tumbled one over the other. Only when soft, inexperienced hooves beat a hopeful ripple in the water, and the smallest bleat and shiver signaled a save, did the candlelit nights exhale.

Assured the young lamb would survive for the present, we wrapped it in cotton towels or table-cloths or, sometimes, depending on how many there had been, in clothes from the closet. One of us, the one still able to walk a straight line and speak with enough clarity to insist upon it, would take the baby lamb back to the sheep barn. My own particular method was to juggle the four long, unwieldy legs deep into my barn coat. Disturbed, a rooster would crow as I shuffled toward the barn. The tiny heart-beat matched my giant one and often I let the lonely baby suck on my chin, chapping it bright red in the frosty air.

Would the ewe remember her offspring? Would she be able to detect its unique smell after hours of bathing in warm water? It was always an operatic re-union, sometimes joyous, sometimes calamitous, and when the outcome was assured, Mother slumped at the kitchen table while I made coffee and cut us both an oversized piece of cake.

It might have been a slice of her specialty, angel food cake, which contained so many fresh egg whites that it baked as high as a cloud. You knew the first time a feathery bite barely clung to your fork why it was called angel food. Or it could have been my golden pound cake, heftily laden with egg yolks and butter and the heady cologne of sweet alfalfa honey. Luscious is a word with few worthy applications, but nothing else describes the cooking that occurred in this kitchen where I now sit, indifferent to food.

I think it's because of that microwave oven that Esther brought over the other day. She unpacked it quickly, plugged it in, and immediately baked a potato the size of Idaho. Suddenly my kitchen is under assault by efficient appliances.

"See?" she said. "Ten minutes, and you won't have to boil a whole pot of water anymore, Miss Irene. Now I can buy a full week's worth of frozen dinners for you at once. It's an absolutely wonderful invention." She put her hand on my arm and lowered her voice. "With your walker to help you get around, you won't need me to fix suppers for you."

She bit her lip and inhaled sharply, as if she'd just accidentally given away a secret. It hadn't occurred to me that Esther might leave, especially not now, when I can see how frail and unhappy she's become.

And I'm not the only one to notice it, either. Reverend Thorne was quite direct. "Miss Irene," he said, stroking that pathetic patch of a beard he calls a goatee, "Does Esther seem nervous to you?"

"Nervous?" I said, "Not nervous, exactly."

"No, that's the wrong word," he said, "But does she seem — upset?"

"Esther Pomeroy is just fine," I said, unwilling to discuss her problems with this exceedingly nosy man, but he opened up a bag of worry just the same.

I'm beginning to think my mind is not as sharp as it once was, because when I asked the Reverend if he would mind trimming back the bushes up in the Leahy cemetery, he said, "Why Miss Irene, I did that three weeks ago when you asked the first time. Can't you see the flowers I planted?"

I leaned across the bed and looked out the window, scanning the upper field where I thought I could see the gravestones, but saw no evidence of landscaping.

"You didn't tell me you did anything," I stuttered.

"I wondered why you didn't mention it."

"Well, anyone can tell it's very nice work, young man," I lied. "I meant to thank you."

Then he ruined the whole moment. "It's God's work," he said, smiling, "And I'm happy to do it."

I may be getting a touch forgetful, but I'll wager that Reverend Thorne's solution to Esther's problems is to pray for her. I have another idea, and I think it's better. She can pack up her children and come to live with me. But I must ask her soon, before she runs away, and I end up at Pine Manor.

WHEN MY FATHER WAS STILL ALIVE, PINE Manor was a combination retirement home and hospital for county residents. It wasn't exactly the "poor house," but it was a clean place to live for men whose homesteads and health had somehow slipped away. It functioned as a working farm, and since nearly everybody who ended up with nothing was a farmer, my father was acquainted with most of them. Some of the machinery and horse tack on our place Father had purchased at their sell-outs. His strongest, most often repeated directive to Mother and me was, "You both hear me now. No matter what happens, never, ever auction the farm. They'll steal you blind and walk away laughing."

We both believed he was right about that, because a good farm auction was the only thing he and Uncle Alton would go out of their way to attend. Oh, I did it along with everyone else — gained some decent equipment that way, too. The buyer's concept of a good auction is based on bidding just high enough to outfinagle your neighbor. Unless the auctioneer knows something you do not — the tractor doesn't have brakes, for example — you can get working machinery, a flock of sheep or herd of cows, feed, tools, and tack at bargain basement prices.

The auction might bring in enough to close out the farmer's accounts. The auctioneer, who takes a commission, and the buyer, who takes the equipment, are the ones who benefit. The farmer, if he's lucky, gets a bag one-third full, a third of the value of his possessions.

The old men who lived at Pine Manor, cracked but not broken, kept a huge garden, milk cows, sheep, hogs, and chickens for meat and eggs. During the year they collected kindling from the surrounding woods so that when the sap started to run in February or March they could tap the six giant sugar maples in front of the building. All day and all night they kept the fire going in the steamy little sugar shack, boiling buckets of the watery sap until enough light amber syrup was made to last a full year. All that remains of those magnificent maples, amputated by an over-anxious chain saw, now are three-foot stumps.

"A safety precaution," some county official explained. "Those trees could fall on the building, cause loss of life, and the county could be liable."

Nonsense.

Years ago, even prisoners were self-reliant, feeding themselves from a communal garden, gaining not only a sense of accomplishment but also the mental and physical health benefits of exercise, fresh air, and sunshine. These days prisoners are robbed of nature and the elderly are stripped of their abilities, planted like potatoes in front of a bingo card.

You can count on this, though. No one is going to ambush me. Esther will not convince me to move into this new, overhauled Pine Manor, nor will Reverend Thorne, no matter how gently he tries to persuade. How can he expect to be taken seriously, anyway, with his pockmarked face and stringy goatee? I might have been a bit unkind when I told him he should shave his face; Esther shot me a look that could have melted a snowman. The next time he comes, I must soften my mouth, nibble instead of bite. But they both must understand that though my body betrays me, my brain has not. I will stay on right here in this house, on this farm, as long as I can sharpen a pencil and write these words.

FINALLY, THERE IS ENOUGH JULY SUN TO dry the soggy earth, and raindrops are not trapped in repetitive streams, chasing each other over and over again from the top of the windowpanes to the bottom. Now I can see the sheep barn at the far side of the yard, how sturdy it still is, how calmly it has withstood slashing storms and tyrannical snowloads. It has not buckled with age, though ground frost has heaved its concrete floor, and the proud red barn boards have aged, like an Irish priest's cheeks, to a polished pearly pink.

More distressed is the chicken coop. In a hard wind it groans like a pregnant cow. Weathered scraps of the shake roof, as light and dry as autumn leaves, flutter to the ground, and its stone foundation is crumbled and weak.

My mother kept a hundred hens in that coop. The birds, teeming with dopey trials and tribulations, were my first introduction to animal husbandry. Because the other livestock required more muscle than a small child could offer, their daily care was left in my six-year-old hands.

Collecting the eggs was a monstrous task for a little girl, and I took the job seriously. I learned early that the famed intuition consigned to women is much more apparent in hens than in people. Somehow, a hen would always know that callously stealing her eggs made me nervous. It was, I thought, only a matter of time before that sharp yellow beak would blind me, or open an enormous gash in the palm of my hand.

Protective as any mother, the hen would stretch her neck out as long as a cobra, jabbing her clawlike beak at my soft skin. Her only weapon, and a flimsy one at that, terrified me. The more excitedly she pecked at me, the more excitedly I jerked and yanked in and out of her nest. We stirred each other into a squawky lather every time.

Effectively, I was of no higher order than a diabolical killer weasel who fastens onto a hen's scrawny neck, sucks her blood, devours her brain, and then for good measure, plunders her egg-laden nest. Childish guilt sometimes bleached justification for my egg-collecting chore. It was, fortunately, the kind of compunction that is salvaged by experience, and over time I learned that mastery of the job required a steady but swift approach. With practice it became easy to confidently slip my hand, palm-down, under the plump mound of blustery red-brown feathers, and pluck the egg like a berry from a bush.

The odd truth is that for the instant before I fled the hen's warm underpinnings, just when my hand closed around a warm, newly deposited egg, it felt alive. The egg was just an egg, of course, not a baby chick, but the thing had the eerie promise of shallow breath. All it needed were some downy, pastel yellow feathers pasted on its pale brown shell.

I remember one evening after I'd collected two or three dozen eggs. The winter sunset, alarming in shades of rose and purple-streaked orange, reflected on the still pond. Up seemed down, down up. Balancing the full basket of eggs on my hip, I reached high above my head to close the chicken coop latch. The personal touch of a brisk breeze stunned me as its icy hand reached under my skirt, and the basket slipped, dropping to the ground. The slushy sound sickened me. Mother, I knew, would be angry, and I stooped to search for any unbroken eggs.

It was then that a nasty rooster I called Clawfoot took a noisy stumble-fly-run vault out of the coop and toward my head. The cock wore the typical defects of the male species like a military officer wears a medal, proudly, with his chest puffed out. Nonchalantly lecherous, yet aloof and in command, Clawfoot's coppery feathers were brighter than a coin collector's penny. Certain his sharp talons would viciously slice my skin, I screamed, and protecting my head with toothpick arms, ran to the house, up the wooden porch steps, straight into my mother's outstretched arms.

That night when she put me to bed, she sang a quiet lullaby about hens and roosters and scared little girls. I wish she had written it down.

A farm without the proud defense or optimistic song of an inflamed rooster is, I fear, one with few promises left in its fields, and as I stare out the window this afternoon, watching the sun move across the roof of the old chicken coop, the distant crow of a confused rooster echoes through the hills. My blankets are twisted around my feet and there is an odd smell. It is me, and I am suddenly, inexplicably lonely.

Chapter Twenty-Four

TOO MANY OBSTACLES, TOO MANY FAIL-
ures, too much hot weather, even too much perfection, can shrivel a person's expectations as
desperately as a cornfield in a drought. People tire,
go stale.

Esther will be here soon and I will give her my
diamond ring. She will make us a pot of tea and
perhaps I will tell her about my engagement to
Maxwell Hunter. I've never told anyone about my
luckless romance. It's a secret I had intended to be
buried along with me, but my Esther could use the
distraction.

I heard her on the telephone yesterday with her
husband. She was hissing like a radiator, so angry at
him that I could not understand what she said. But
I did hear her tell him to "stay in bed, then, just you
stay in bed all day long."

She flung the phone down as if it were hot metal.
"Damn him, Miss Irene. Just damn him and his
garage and his greasy little friends who come into

my house and drink beer all day long." And then, embarrassed, she ran outside.

I remember when Michael opened his car repair shop; Esther was as excited as a bride. She vibrated with expectation. She'd invested hundreds of dollars in his project — savings it had taken years to accumulate — and all of this just months away from motherhood.

Some men drink colorless liquor as if they were actually thirsty, and Michael is one of them. They suck on bottles to cushion their self-knowledge. They know they could dehydrate and die, and the ashen coat of disappointment worn by their sad-faced women doesn't help a bit. Children study the downfall of their parents, but instead of mastering the lesson, they take the same route, failing even more spectacularly. Esther had hoped that she would be able to turn the horse around, change the course of Michael's history, but she cannot.

I will not lie about alcohol. Prohibition held no authority out in the country where Yankee stills were easy to find. Only the women of the Christian Temperance League denied themselves a taste of dandelion wine. Hard apple cider the color of gasoline has burned my tongue, and more than one garnet glass of elderberry wine has sweetened my lips, but never more than once a week, and never to excess. Mother would have a holiday glass of mulled red wine, too, or a small taste of Father's homemade brew. It's no surprise that even God-fearing people find at least pleasure, if not salvation, in drink.

One time, a neighbor spilled a whole wagon full of hay on some loose gravel at the top of Pike Road. The dogs started such a ruckus that I dropped a basket of onions on the floor and ran to the gun cabinet, thinking that the sheep surely were in trouble. But instead of coyotes, I found Bill Birdsall standing in the yard like a dazed scarecrow, blood from a cut in his head soaking his overalls. He thanked me mightily for a taste of my whiskey that day.

There's still an old half-empty bottle of whiskey somewhere in the cupboard. I mix a tablespoon with honey to medicate a sore throat or swallow a cupful to ease a misadventure. There must be some jars of parsnip or dandelion wine stored in the cellar, too, by now hidden in cobwebs and dust, good wine gone to vinegar.

ESTHER SAYS ALCOHOL BURNS HER MOUTH, and she will not take a drink. She's a bit like the hens — vulnerable in a feisty sort of way. Nearly everything gobbles up an unprotected chicken, and my Esther is unprotected, targeted like the chickens, for trouble.

From the hazardous sky swoop of her own egg-laying cousins to the most sophisticated New York restaurant, hens are fair game. Add the lady of the house's kill knife, her stew pot sitting at the ready, and even the most hardened human might commiserate with the trials of the barnyard chicken.

The weasel is the worst, I think. In winter, he changes color, turning white to match the snow. Esther called her own husband a weasel once, laughing not with cheer, but with the dispirited voice of an unlucky gambler.

Perhaps this afternoon I will tell her about when a weasel got into Mother's chickens, but I sense my ability to distract her is failing. When she came yesterday, she would not stop for my story about Maxwell.

I said, "Esther, sit with me awhile, will you? I have a story to tell you."

But she was in a hurry. "I can't stay today, Miss Irene," she said. "I have to take Mikey for a check-up." And once again her eyes filled up like a cup of water, but she would not tell me what was the matter.

Even when I said, "What is wrong, dear? Can I help?" she turned away and shook her head.

Esther should listen to me. She should listen, but I know she will have no time to hear about what happened when the weasel got into the chicken coop.

It was Father's last summer, the summer of my seventeenth year. Three evenings in a row the varmint had killed some of the best laying hens and decimated the eggs. It was on the fourth evening, during that curt moment before total darkness, when the sky soaks into the ground, that the chickens suddenly made an extraordinary racket.

"That weasel made a big mistake tonight!" I yelled, dropping the dish towel, grabbing the kerosene lamp, and running into the chicken coop. I was determined to turn the tables on the beast, and my father was right behind me, armed with a coal shovel.

Bravely, I held the lamp high searching each corner of the coop. The birds were more than agitated; they were deranged with fright. But the kerosene lamp cast our monstrous shadows on the walls, and, like people, chickens can be shocked into near silence. Those that had flown up in panic to the ceiling flapped gently to keep balance on the unfamiliar rafters. They watched the patterns the light threw on the walls with the glassy black eyes of the doomed.

Chickens do have short attention spans, however, and as we stood still, searching for the weasel, they began to chirp and chatter, murmuring sadly at the wake of a child. A dangerous enemy had penetrated their walls. That they had no hope of self-defense, much less retaliation, aroused in me a furious need to guard them. I heard myself grunting like a trapped soldier, when suddenly I pointed to the far corner of the coop.

"There he is," I whispered. "Give me the shovel." I surely saw the weasel, whiskers alert, black eyes indecipherable. The dark animal ignited my own murderous flame. I was ready to kill.

"Just hold on now, Reeni," Father said. "I'll get him for you."

Our shadows, tall and slender on the walls, quivered.

I conceded and held the inadequate light high.

Father raised the flat end of the shovel above his head, prepared to divide the long-limbed, cowering beast in two.

"Whoa." With the concentration of a telepathic, he halted his motion.

"This isn't the weasel, damn it. It's the hen, goddamnit, and she's still breathing."

Father grabbed the light from me, holding it inches above the pathetic creature. He thrust out his right arm, banging my breasts with the privilege of pure protection.

"Stay back," he spit, pushing me away.

But I had already seen the dark red damage. Indeed, the body of the chicken was still deeply inhaling and exhaling, but she was headless, a decapitated breathing body.

"How can she still be alive?" I asked. Irrationally, grade school history lessons and images of the French Revolution floated in front of me. I dropped to my knees, bending over the body. I leaned in close enough to smell the hen's fresh flowing blood, close enough to feel its gummy thickness on the tip of my nose.

As the hen took her last wheezing breaths, Father pulled me away. But like a puppy at a slipper, I resisted, clipping tightly onto his pant leg.

Gradually, the muted sound of a single violin filled

the chicken coop. Father and I both dropped to the sawdust-covered floor and leaned over the hen. I placed my ear close to her warm throbbing body. The music, louder now, and clearer, was coming from her.

"Get up, Reeni," Father whispered, tugging my arm.

There was a sudden rush of motion under the wire-draped window and the weasel made his slick escape. He moved fast, causing a tunnel of sawdust to follow him as he slid out of a small opening in the rock foundation. As quickly as an accident, the hens began to flap and fly, kicking up the dust and a terrible uproar. I kneeled over the headless hen, waiting. She took her deepest breath, and the music stopped.

Father held the lifeless body upside down by the feet as we backed out of the blood-splashed chicken coop. With a mighty heave, he threw her into the high brush behind the building. Some meat-eating animal stalking mice in the tall red pokeweed and indomitable burdocks would find the carcass. By winter, the hard bleached bones would remain in the tangle of high dried grass, sharp as used arrows and useless.

I was trembling as Father and I headed back to the house. Water gently rippled in the pond as we passed. Maybe that was the music I heard. Maybe a sudden breeze had churned the water, making a sound like a violin. Maybe the breeze caused the giant bull thistles growing on the dike to graze against one another. Could that have created the music I heard in the chicken coop?

Finally, I mustered the courage to ask my father, "Did you hear anything in there?"

It was too dark to see his face, but I could feel his gaze. It took a long time for him to answer and I listened to the lapping water.

"The music, Reeni? Did you hear a violin?"

"I think so."

"I don't know what it means, Reeni. I've heard it twice before."

Stunned, I sat down on the back porch steps. Father took a deep breath and sat down beside me. The surface of the pond shimmered under the full, observant moon; ghostly pearls of light floated gently, rolling to the edges of the huge spring-fed bowl like beads of unleashed mercury.

Chapter Twenty-Five

THAT NIGHT, MY FATHER AND I PERCHED
on the edge of the porch steps like nervous birds.
Father's demeanor was on the grim side of serious,
but I could not suppress a suspicion that this was
all a joke. He gnawed on the end of a long blade of
poverty grass, a useless early spring grass, unpalat-
able to cows and sheep, but good for men to chew
while pondering life's mysteries. The strain of the
long day was audible in his deep breath. I looked at
his face, ghostly and waxen in the moonlight. His
toothy, relaxed smile was gone. My scalp itched and
my lower eyelid twitched like a colt's ear.

This night of revelation turned out to be only
weeks away from Father's final breath and, like
many men who depend on their women to nurse and
nurture, to watch for hazardous pitfalls, he was unlucky. He did not have a shrewd wife, an attentive
daughter. We were all taken by surprise, despite the
many clues. Now, he coughed, cleared his throat,
coughed again as the round, unblinking eye of the

sky gazed coldly at the pond, which stared back, steadily.

It was a grave moon, neither romantic nor beautiful, the kind that convened coyotes and frightened horses. It made me pull my shirt tightly around my shoulders and huddle on the step.

Father sighed as deeply as his lungs allowed and looked up at the second floor of the house. Mother appeared briefly at the bedroom window, then fussing with a pillow slip, moved out of sight. A kerosene lamp flickered in the window. We watched as she reappeared, turned down the bed, fluffed the pillows and, like a little girl in her freshly laundered nightgown, climbed in.

Sucking his blade of grass, pacing in small circles, Father pointed at the bedroom window and whispered, "Let's talk down by the pond."

I felt uneasy, even with my father, for it was a large body of water and a fully inhabited universe. Even as a child on a hot summer's day, I had been afraid to swim. Snakes and snappers lived in that pond. At night, it especially frightened me, and I was surprised that Father would take me to its edge, because he knew I was leery of its black water. The safe shallow rim was my limit, beyond that ankle-deep threshold there was no bottom, no way to hold onto the earth. No, I was not a swimmer, not one to release my toehold on the land, to challenge the snapper's primordial jaws with my soft flesh.

Now I move the curtain by this bed aside and I

see it, a classic pond; large, but not as large as I believed when I was a girl, round and framed by high grass and cattails. Tree swallows are swooping inches above its flat unwrinkled face, dining on mosquitoes. From below the hungry trout crack its glassy ceiling, vying for the same mosquitoes. All of this activity I watch from my bed, motionless. The pond binds me to truth, leads me to meditation, and the past rises and rises until I am exhausted with memory.

AS I FOLLOWED FATHER ACROSS THE YARD, the resolute moon rose higher, its yellow and blotchy face reflecting on the water. Standing on the bank, we listened to the ripples licking sloppily at our feet. Father dropped to one knee and looked past me into the darkness, his normally robust and confident voice now as quiet as a funeral usher's.

"I can only tell you what I know, Reeni — what's happened to me, and please don't ask me to explain any of it. I heard that violin music twice before in my life. Remember me telling you about my first buck? I was sixteen or seventeen, about your age. He was a beauty, twelve points with a perfect rack. Your Uncle Alton was hunting with me, but he was sitting a tree stand on the other side of the hill. You know the place — down in the hemlocks where the stone walls cross."

I did know the place. It was right there that just a week before I had seen a porcupine amble along the meandering wall. I didn't interrupt Father, but my interest was already waning. With an expertly practiced side-arm pitch, I started to throw stones across the water. Three, four, maybe five times, they would splash and bounce before heavily sinking thirty feet, never again to be warmed by the sun.

Finally, Father grabbed my arm, hurting it. "Quit it, Reeni," he said. "This is important. The buck fell about a mile south of town. I knew I'd hit him in the neck, but he was one bullheaded beast and I had to track him. There was a lot of blood and there was just enough snow to help me out. Must have been about two inches on the ground."

I remained quiet, not daring to move.

"The deer was still alive, just like that hen tonight. The slug had gone right through his neck, nicking the jugular. That's when I heard the music. I thought something had happened to my eardrum, but the closer I got to the buck the louder it became."

Now I knew I could speak, and my voice trembled. "Was it the same music? Violin music?" I did not know very much about classical music, and though I had a good singing voice, my knowledge of the violin was limited to Uncle Alton's foot-stomping fiddle. But this music was slightly familiar, like something I may have heard on a Victrola — passionate, complicated, intensely beautiful.

"It was the same music," Father answered. "I got down on my hands and knees and put my ear right on the wound. Got blood all over myself for doing it, too. I'm telling you, Reeni, and I've never told another soul, violin music came right out of that buck, right from the wound. It didn't stop until he took his last breath."

I was stunned. "You've never told anybody, not even Mother?"

"No, no. I didn't say anything about it to anyone. I figured it was something I just imagined, some trick of the mind. I did want to bury that carcass deep, but we couldn't afford to waste a whole year's venison. Anyhow, your Uncle Alton heard my shot and showed up a few minutes later to help do the field dressing."

"You said you heard the music twice," I said, backing on wobbly knees away from the water's edge.

"I'm going to tell you this fast, Reeni," Father said. "Your brother didn't die like Mother and I told you."

He gazed across the silver surface of the pond. A fish splashed.

"What did you say?" I was certain I'd misunderstood.

"Your mother and I don't know exactly how it happened, but I found him here, floating." Father pointed to the pond.

I listened to Father with my head tilted, like a dog trying to understand a new command.

"I'd been shearing the sheep and came up to the house for dinner," he said. "He was floating at the edge, Reeni, face down. I dragged his little body onto the bank. His heart was still beating."

For the first time I heard a catch in my father's voice, and the slow ribbon of tears squeezing from the corner of his eyes shimmered in the moonlight. "Four years old, Reeni, and I forgot to watch out for him. I had gotten used to him, because he followed me all over this farm. He was a strange little boy, in some ways. He never cried. I had gotten used to him the way you get used to your little finger. You were only two. You don't remember that day, do you Reeni?"

His eyes burned into mine. A washed-out memory of my mother burst into color. She was standing in the yard, reaching up high, her long yellow skirt ballooning in the breeze. I was sitting on the ground next to a basket of laundry. A few faded dresses dangled on the line, and then I remembered Father's face, so contorted I barely recognized him as he ran toward us from the pond. Billy's body flopped in his arms and water dripped from their clothes, sprinkling the grass like a fine spring rain.

" 'He's breathing, he's still breathing', I hollered to your mother, and we pushed his chest in and out. I crushed his tiny ribs trying to bring him back." Now Father was sobbing openly, but my own emotions were more controlled. I felt curiously removed, even, one might say, cold, and less interested in my brother's death than on how the event had affected my life.

"That's the second time I heard the violin, Reeni," he finally whispered. "I put my ear right onto his lips

211

and I heard music, just like tonight, just like when I shot the buck. But your mother didn't. She was wailing, clawing at Billy, slapping his face, pounding his body as if to force life back into him. The sounds that came from your mother that night haunt me to this day, Reeni. Finally, she sank to her knees, understanding, and she held him in her arms, rocking, rocking, rocking, but the music had already stopped. She never heard anything.

Father, his face contorted in the moonlight, picked up a rock and threw it at the pond with a vengeance. The water gulped loudly, and he said no more until the splash subsided. "You crawled under the porch and wouldn't come out. Your Uncle Alton stayed there with you until you fell asleep."

NOW I UNDERSTOOD THOSE LAZY SUMMER afternoons when I was a girl, spread out flat on the splintery dock, careful not to touch the water. Dreamily, I would watch the iridescent blue damselflies ornament the cattails and the flitty water striders, too delicate to be called bugs, go about their busy day. While the sun browned the back of my knees, I studied the salamanders that pointlessly hung motionless just under the water's surface. Then, drowsy with the heat, I would concentrate on my reflection, but never did the face seem to be my own. Its mouth was unfamiliar, its unblinking eyes odd and vacant.

Now I understood.

It was Billy looking back at me, and no longer was the pond a dark and hungry hole, for it meant that I would never really be left alone. And I knew why my parents had lied about Billy's death. It was their method of protecting their last child, their baby girl. A bond of grief at first, a holy secret, and then a forgotten one.

I thought of the turkey hunt with Father, and how he explained to my mother that there would be no guns. I thought of how I begged for the kind of rifle Annie Oakley used, and how Mother shattered a plate on the kitchen counter when Father agreed to buy it for my twelfth birthday. And I remembered the times I was sick in bed with a common childhood fever, the way my mother's face was pale and distraught, as if Death had come to take me, too.

Chapter Twenty-Six

"I DON'T FEEL VERY WELL TODAY," I TOLD Esther. "My skin hurts like sunburn." She did not reply. "You didn't come yesterday. You didn't even call. All night long I worried."

She rubbed her eyes and sighed. "Miss Irene, you are really something, you are. When did you start whining? You're starting to sound like Mike. I told you I had to take Mikey, Jr. to the doctor yesterday, didn't I? But now I'm going to rub your feet until you go to sleep, and I'll be back to see you first thing in the morning. I want to talk to Reverend Thorne tomorrow, too," she said.

I settled back into the pillows, but the feel of her hands sliding up and down one foot then the other did not put me to sleep. Sleep is for those who have more time. The agony of aging is known only to the old, and we keep quiet lest our keepers grow resentful that we're still alive.

I must give Esther my ring soon, but I want to have the proper amount of time. I want to tell her about

Maxwell, about how even a walnut like me once had love.

But she should telephone if she's not coming, give me some notice. She knows I'm not fond of the telephone, but still, she could have called. Lately, the phone rings too much, invading my sleep, demanding my attention, which is in short supply. When finally I roll over, struggling to wrap my seized fingers around the receiver, I'm connected to a stranger who offers me life insurance or a credit card, vinyl siding and bay windows. The telephone is a device that nurses charlatans.

And now, on the days that he doesn't drive all the way out here, Reverend Thorne has taken to calling me, too. I wouldn't mind having a decent talk with the man, but he is not a very good conversationalist.

He always starts off the same way: "Good morning, Miss Leahy. This is Reverend Thorne. And how are you this blessed day?" And that's the last question he asks about me. The next five minutes are spent in a blather of news about Holy Christ Church, sprinkled with a reference or two to Pine Manor Home.

Even though Esther tells me I need a hearing aid, I'm sure she's wrong because I can hear the preacher's high-pitched voice just fine. It's as annoying as a yapping chihuahua. I would trade the last ten years of my life if just once Joe would put his paws up on the side of this bed and talk to me. If any dog could talk, it would be a border collie, and it would be an intelligent conversation, too, not meandering like a beagle's or dumb like a basset hound's.

I don't need to hear the Reverend Thorne any better than I already do, and I do not want a hearing aid stuck like a button in my ear. Everyone knows right away that you have a problem, so they start screaming, and before you know it you really are deaf.

For me, the telephone is a tool to access necessities. If a storm knocks out the electricity you can call Mohawk Electric, or you can call in an order to Sears for a new set of bed sheets, or if the house catches fire you can call the fire department.

Mother used to love to ring Evie Dalton. They talked to each other every day, if only to compare thermometers.

"Temperature reads minus fifteen up here, Evie," Mother would say into the mouthpiece. Then she'd turn to me, put her hand over the phone, roll her eyes, and in a stage whisper say, "Evie Dalton claims its minus seventeen down in the hollow."

Sometimes I wish I had an Evie Dalton to call, but I've never been much of a chatterer.

It's perfectly all right with me if Esther can't lift her little finger to dial the telephone. She was snappier than the meanest turtle today.

"Why didn't you call *me*, Miss Irene? You have my number. The phone works two ways, you know, and I can't *always* be worrying about your egg salad."

She didn't mean that last.

"I don't even feel like *thinking* about your egg

salad right now, Miss Irene, if that's all right with you. Everything's been going wrong lately, and now Mikey has asthma, and the pre-school says Skeeter needs a psychiatrist."

She looked at the floor while I stared in disbelief.

"How can those sappy little teachers determine that?" I demanded. Most of those people are not even a quarter of my age and I'd guess that their wisdom is still tinted green.

"They tested her," she said. "They gave her a whole battery of tests after she refused to talk."

"Refused to talk?" I squealed.

Now I know that my Esther takes good care of her children, and that weasel of a husband, too. There's nary a dog hair left on my floor after she vacuums; no streaks in the windows, and she must be feeding me — I'm puffier than a bowl of popped corn, although Esther says that's because of my new medicine. But like Esther told me, I'm perfectly able to rise from this bed, persuade my legs to move to the walker, and microwave myself a decent meal.

The woman is obviously overly stressed and after our little spat, I saw her slumped at the kitchen table, crying. Tension rubs off on dogs like dust on glass, and Joe whimpered and pawed my light summer sheet onto the floor. It cut my afternoon nap in two, but Esther did not notice. I kept my eyes open just a slit and watched.

She held her head in her hands like a bowl, and her whole body seemed to shimmy from the inside out. Tears slipped through her slim fingers, rolling in a brown path down to her elbows. She had been cleaning the cupboards; the wash rag soaked in Murphy's Oil Soap lay on the floor like a sleeping gray squirrel. Finally, she lowered her hands and sighing deeply, wiped her slick, bloated face with a tea towel. The pause should have changed her direction. Instead, she crumpled again, sobbing.

One thing I've learned about women is that usually they don't cry in each other's kitchens unless there is trouble with a man. When Esther finally quit, she washed her hands, drew herself a glass of water and took two aspirin. I wanted to talk to her, but my spying had trapped me into silence, and when Esther quietly approached my bed and picked up my notebook, I still kept my eyes closed, not tightly like a child pretending to sleep, but convincingly shut. I even snorted a small snore as she turned away and sat back down at the table.

Now, I thought. Now is when I will witness the prying I suspected all along. How wrong an old lady can be.

Esther merely needed a piece of paper, and she pulled it out of the spiral bound book noiselessly. After she'd finished writing, she placed the book back where she found it on my bed, set out my evening pills, and leaned the note against the lamp so it would be the first thing I would see when I awoke, which was, naturally, the minute she slipped out of the door.

"Dear Miss Irene," she had written, "I'm sorry to

have to leave while you're still asleep. Be sure to take your medicine before you turn in for the night. There's a frozen meatloaf dinner in the freezer — the microwave is all set, just press the red button. I will be back in the morning for your bath. Sleep well, dear."

Upstairs, there are three bedrooms. The one at the top of the landing is where I was born, with a southern exposure and three windows that go from the floor to the ceiling. Esther can have that room when she comes to live with me. The other two are smaller, but surely as large as anything a double-wide can offer. Little Mike and Skeeter will like them.

When Esther lives here, I'll ask her to get out the old photo albums. She'll put her children to bed, then sit next to me, and I'll tell her the story of each picture. I will see my garden growing again and taste the tomatoes and corn, and the tall grass will sway in the fields, and the sheep will answer one another, their pensive bleats lingering in the air like the scent of wild flowers.

TONIGHT FOR SUPPER I HAD THE MEATLOAF and mashed potato concoction, with mushy peas and carrots for added color — no threat to any fresh vegetables I've ever tasted. I would have liked my normal glass of milk, but these gnarled old hands can't lift the jug. I need Esther for that.

My God. I need Esther for everything.

Chapter Twenty-Seven

HONEST SLEEP WAS SCORNFUL LAST night, shunning me as if to punish my deceit. Moonlight skated across my white sheets, silver stars glittered against the black velvet sky, and all night I watched them through my window, waiting to join the darkness. And when it did not come I allowed myself the luxury of imagination, and about the bath Esther will give me today.

When she leans across the bed to lift my arms, she smells like my mother, fresh and sweet as a lilac bush in bloom. I endured many a sponge bath before I was able to enjoy them without embarrassment, but now I lean back relaxed as a kitten. Esther is settled, unrushed, and the bath water is warm, the sponge a gentle massage. Carefully, she cradles my head with one strong arm, washing my hair in the basin of water until it squeaks like a vinegar-washed, newspaper-dried picture window. She wraps my head in a hard, clean towel and she dries between my toes, behind my knees, always with respect. She splashes lavender on my lacy-veined skin, and I arrange myself between the air-dried sheets as clean and fresh as a soft-skinned baby.

The accoutrements of an old farm lady's vanity are usually confined to her tidy, productive kitchen, her hair, not cut short like mine but often braided and top-knotted, and perhaps, her hands. The futility of transforming the two sunburned and chapped, cracked and leathery workhorses into the elegant hands advertised in the magazines can be measured by the array of creams and lotions for sale in the stores. Even my father's hands were softer than mine, a combination of constantly handling the lanolin-laden sheep and an unfamiliarity with dish and laundry soap.

Stupidly, I ignored my own youthful beauty, the blushing, soft skin, the full lips and breasts. I did not ladle preservative creams and potions onto my body, nor did I wear wide-brimmed hats to evade the skin-parching sun. Too late, it became apparent how rapidly that which is luscious about a woman's body spoils like forgotten fruit.

Esther takes better care of herself, rubbing globs of cream into her hands until it disappears, touching her mouth lightly with pink lipstick. She brings pastel bottles of new shampoos to try on my hair, and apple-scented rinses that leave it soft and untangled. Lately, she's taken to singing soft hymns when she washes me — *Amazing Grace, Nearer My God to Thee* — old familiar songs that even I can recognize. She does not mention Pine Manor or Reverend Thorne.

It is a consideration I value and when the time is right, I will give her the ring as a token of my appreciation. When she comes to live with me, I will give each of the children a welcome gift, too, something to cherish. I will crawl one more time up to the attic, for surely a treasure awaits them there.

IT WAS ALREADY EIGHT O'CLOCK WHEN I heard Esther's pickup rattle into the driveway. My walker and I were working our way across the kitchen toward the microwave. Usually by this time I've already had my instant oatmeal and Esther has cleaned up the kitchen, but not this morning.

The truck door slammed hard and Joe barked once, managing a weak wag when she came inside. Esther's eyes were red-rimmed and bulging.

"Here, here," she said, rushing to me. "Let me get that for you, Miss Irene." She took the bowl of oatmeal out of my hands, and helped me to the kitchen table. "I'll get you the milk," she said. "I'm sorry I'm late this morning. Things . . . things got out of hand at home."

It felt good to have breakfast at the kitchen table, instead of on a tray in bed. Esther fixed both of us a cup of tea and sat across from me.

Years washed away. Suddenly, I was a strong

woman again. I straightened my posture, held my cup of tea graciously in front of me. Esther unfolded her long limbs carefully, as if a sudden motion would tear them off her body like tissue paper. She clasped her hands in her lap, stared at the floor, and said nothing.

I let her be, sipping my tea.

Finally, I thought, Esther was going to confide in me. I'm sure she has been consulting with Reverend Thorne. Just the other day, I saw the two of them pacing back and forth in the driveway. He was his comfortable self in his khaki shorts, but even in the midday sun Esther had crossed her arms on her chest, looking chilly in a sleeveless blue dress. Neither of them seemed happy and Esther's head was bowed, talking to the preacher a mile a minute.

As we sat together at the old kitchen table, I realized that the time had come to invite Esther to live with me. I was sure she would accept. Then I would open my arms wide and we would hug, and, perhaps with tears in both of our eyes, we would agree that the children could choose which of the upstairs bedrooms they wanted. My old bedroom would be hers. We would get a puppy for the children, a border collie, or any old mutt they could find. Children are wizards at finding stray puppies.

Just as I was about to speak, Esther took a long breath and said, "Miss Irene, I've got to tell you something. I'm leaving Mike."

A foul infection was under control and I smiled,

encouraging her. Joe's nose poked between her knees from under the table and he licked her salty fingers. She fumbled with his ears. The dog had taken to Esther right from the start and now, as the first of many more tears began to fall, he was worried about her.

"You and Reverend Thorne are the only ones who know about this, Miss Irene. You've got to promise not to tell anyone."

I nodded.

Esther leaned across the table, taking both of my hands in hers. "Miss Irene, I'm going to Atlanta to stay with my sister Roxanne for a while."

More than her words, her tone stunned me into silence. It was as firm as oak and I knew instantly that it would take some adroit maneuvering to get her to agree to my idea.

"Your sister can take you and the children? She has room for all three?"

"I'm leaving the kids here, with my mother. I'm going alone. To my sister in Georgia. Alone."

"You can't do that, Esther," I protested. "It's backwards, all backwards. You don't leave your children. They leave you. That's poor mothering, Esther, and you're a good mother. I used to cull ewes for poor mothering. They ended up in the slaughterhouse, for heaven's sake."

My heart was beating like a hummingbird's wings, but Esther wasn't listening to me. "It's just temporary, until I can send for them. I need to be alone right now." Then, in a low, tortured chant she intoned, "Alone. Away. Alone. Away."

She was rubbing Joe's ears so hard that finally he whimpered in pain, lighting a small flame of reality in Esther's eyes.

"Mike doesn't know a thing about this, and he won't be able to trace the ticket, because Reverend Thorne bought it for me. He paid for it himself, Miss Irene, and said I could repay him later." For the briefest moment, the tense lines around her mouth softened, then returned, furrowing even deeper. "But Mike might call you, Miss Irene. Please, please, please don't talk to him. My own mother doesn't even know yet, but she'll have the sheriff on him if he shows up at her place. She's seen him drunk."

"Your mother doesn't know you're leaving the children with her?"

Esther unraveled like a ball of twine. She cradled her head in her arms. Tears darkened the long brown sleeves of her blouse under which I supposed there were fresh bruises. I'd never before noticed the pale freckles on the back of her hands, brown sugar sifted onto white skin. She looked like a fawn lost in the woods.

"Esther, listen to me," I said, loudly, struggling out of the scarred kitchen chair. The pain that lives in my bent bones dissolved and I stood solidly erect as Esther leaned on me, sobbing. I stroked her hair, her arms, rested her head against my breast.

More quietly, so as not to scare her away, I said again, "Esther, dear, listen to me. You and Skeeter and little Mikey can live here with me. It will be fine."

It was as if I had placed a burning coal in her hand and instantly she pulled away. She stared into my eyes with disbelief. Slowly, like snow in rain, she dissolved into laughter. In the moving pictures of my mind, I saw my Esther smiling happily as she painted Skeeter's room a girlish rosebud pink. I saw little Mikey playing with the turkey feather I planned to give him, and in a powerful voice I victoriously shouted, "We won't have to worry about that bastard ever again!"

Chapter Twenty-Eight

IT CERTAINLY HAS BEEN A DEVILISH SUM-
mer. What with the rain and losing Esther, my life
is more jumbled than before. Reverend Thorne tells
me her children are with her now in Atlanta. She
writes to him once a week, he says, and always asks
about me. I would write her a letter, but her address
is a secret. As chatty as the Reverend is, he will not
give it to me. "We don't want her husband to come
around bothering you for it, Miss Irene," he tells me,
patting my hand as if that would help.

He knows I miss my Esther. I think he might miss
her, too.

At least the last time I saw her she was laughing.
And crying at the same time, too. We both were. I
suppose it was a silly old woman's notion, having her
come to live with me.

After I offered, and she had wiped her eyes, she
told me how much she loved me. "Oh, Miss Irene
Constantine Leahy," she said, almost crooning my
name, "You are a piece of work, and I love you

dearly." Then she laughed again and seemed stronger, as if she had traveled as far into the depths as she was about to go.

"Well," I said, feeling a bit weak myself, but relieved to see her smiling again, "Well, it was just an idea."

We hugged again for a long time, and while she stroked my hair, I slipped Maxwell's ring into her pocket.

THE SOCIAL SERVICES SENT ANOTHER NEW girl to replace Esther. I tell them no one can replace Esther, that they should just quit trying, but still they send various shapes and sizes of women over like cargo.

This one's name is Donna. She has my mother's closed-mouth smile and for the same reason — brown and broken teeth. She set up her own big black radio with loudspeakers that bellow rock and roll in the kitchen. She speaks to me like I'm a baby. She speaks to me like some people talk to their parakeets, pursing her lips in my face, coating her words with artificial sweetener: "Here you go, Irene, have a little bite of your lunch now."

Then, before I even get a good look at the food, she whisks away the whole plate, feigning disappointment: "Must be you're not hungry." It's a lesson she wants to teach me, because I like to take my time with my dinner.

I don't have to worry about my notebooks with

her, though. I know Esther must have read them, but there's a blank look on this one's slack face, a look that says she reads nothing but the *TV Guide.* To be frank, this Donna person puts me in mind of an overweight ewe. She's the third one to come here since Esther left. Both of the others were allergic to dogs, for heaven's sake.

Word must be spreading that I've gone daft. The opposite, in fact, is true. The walker is abandoned, standing like a leggy fiend in the corner of the parlor. My hooked wooden cane sufficiently steadies me. An odd influx of energy boils through my veins. Sometimes, I am flushed with its intensity, ready to walk Pike Road again, hike in the woods where the chickadees are waiting to land on my hand.

I want to walk up the hill through the apple orchard, where my family lies under the trees. From the living room window, I can see now where Reverend Thorne has been tending the flowers, cutting back the weeds and trimming the poverty grass from the gravestones. He does it every week. I detect a certain amount of pride in the job — I should have him review the seven deadly sins for me.

The cool fingers of September are tracing chilly lines up and down my back. Soon the verdant sugar maples will shift to ribald red and orange, like giant torches on the hillsides. Conga drums should accompany their wild display as doomed leaves the size of a lumberjack's hand finally yield.

This autumn, that rushed but passionate season, is my ninety-first.

Chapter Twenty-Nine

IT OCCURRED TO ME THIS MORNING WHILE I was buttering my toast — Donna gave it to me dry as a bone — that my death is actually near. I feel oddly confident that my ninety-first birthday will pass in January just as surely as the seasons, but lurking on the pages of the year's new calendar is a numbered square that will be my last day.

Like my eyes, which were once as blue as the darkest iris but have faded now to the color of chipped ice, winter this year will lose its sparkling hue. I cannot look forward to the warmth of the wood fire or the glimpse of a spread-winged cardinal, an artist's red splash on the snow-white canvas. Pine Manor waits for me to drop into its bowels like a sinner into the pit of hell. But I am not a sinner, nor am I quite ready to die: my pencil remains as sharp as the thorn of a rose.

* * *

LATELY I'VE BEEN ATTRACTING PEOPLE like bugs to potatoes. Strangers are stripping me, invading my privacy, telling me what to do. Every realtor in Carniff County has knocked on this door. One blue-suited young lady suggested that I paint the house before putting it on the market, and, she added, "A new roof wouldn't hurt either."

"What makes you think I'm putting it on the market?" I asked. "Do you know something I don't?"

She blushed and backed down the porch steps. "I heard you wanted to sell."

A man from Red Ruby Real Estate came to talk to me about selling the farm, too. I had to laugh. He galloped into this house with two gold chains draped around his neck and some kind of turquoise bracelet on his wrist.

"Miss Leahy," he said, bellowing like a lovesick cow, "I'd like to be the first person you call when you decide to sell this place." He leaned into my face, hovering over my bed like a hawk. "And don't you let that McFee auctioneer in here either," he said, spotting the pamphlet McFee sent to me last week. "I've got buyers up the gumpstump and can get you a good price. You don't need an auctioneer to sell off this eighty-five acres. Just take a look out of your window, Miss Leahy. Development has come to Donohue Flats and you're in on the ground floor." He grinned at me.

Well, I may not need an auctioneer to sell my place, but I surely don't need this fellow, either. I've been watching the tips of those new houses out of my window for a month now. All I need to do is move the curtain just a tad to the left and four new rooftops peek through the trees like triangular eyes, staring over on this side of the ridge.

The realtor looked around the corner of the stone fireplace into the kitchen and then around the hearth, up the stairs and to the second floor. Joe stood still as a stone right behind him. There's nothing like the seat-level teeth of a growling dog to test a man's nerves.

"You bring an auctioneer in here and you'll lose a lot of money, Miss Leahy." His eye fell to the desk in the kitchen, the desk where my father studied his books on apples, the desk where I paid feed bills and wrote my letters to the editor of *Farm Journal.* It's just a pine table really, but probably two hundred years old.

"You should let me take a look at your furniture." He laughed. "You know, I sell everything on this round earth. Got lots of connections, too. I could get you a better price for this place than anyone else, bar none. I'll guarantee that. Farm this size, could gain you thirty, maybe forty thousand dollars. Set you up for the rest of your life, Miss Leahy. You won't have to worry about a thing."

Forty thousand. Mr. Red Ruby paid more than that for his car, maybe more than that for the gold chain that hangs around his suntanned neck, but I didn't even raise my voice. I said I'd think about it and would telephone him when I was ready to sell.

232

Joe's patience broke as the man retreated out the back door. Joyfully, he nipped at the agent's ankles. I should have scolded the old dog, but we both knew a reprimand would have been false.

Then Adelaide Malcolm marched into my house and announced that the church was looking for donations. "It's time for the annual flea market and I just know you have a houseful of things you'll need to get rid of. I wanted to get to you before the Fire Department does. Their auction is coming up soon."

After Father died, Mother warned me about such invaders.

"Be careful, Reeni," she told me. "Never let anyone barge into the house. Always step outside to talk, and know where your gun is." She was also a fan of snappish, unfriendly dogs. Lost outsiders who often stopped for directions to the Balsam Campgrounds were greeted with a face of marble when they approached my mother. She'd glare at the canoe-topped car and its occupants long enough to make them nervous, then give the directions all right, but in an icy monotone that said don't come back this way.

I'm going to have to take her advice.

Mutton-faced Donna is insufferable and mean. When her own fat feet accidentally kicked my notebook far under the bed where it lay in deep dust and doghair, she refused to retrieve it. Later I asked her again, louder. She could have a hearing problem, I reckoned, but she answered, "You don't have to yell, Irene," then continued to read her *National Enquirer.*

I was so upset I couldn't get her attention that I knocked my glass of milk off of the bed tray, which didn't help matters. She didn't even look up when it splashed all over the floor. Now the milk is souring. Luckily for me, smell is right up there with sight and sound when it comes to the decline of the senses. I do get a whiff now and then; it's the familiar aroma of barns and cows and dairymen's clothes. Joe has wiggled under the bed and become obsessed with licking the floor. I suppose he's well enough equipped to do the required cleaning; I just wish he could fetch that notebook.

Donna hasn't vacuumed once, and the clusterflies are accumulating in piles under the windows. Every time I remind her, she says she'll do it tomorrow, or she laughs and says her place has twice as many as mine. Slow-moving and smaller than regular houseflies, clusterflies have inefficient tapered wings, not meant for much flying. Hundreds of them gather in tight groups under the clapboards of the house or in dark places where only an insect can thrive. They don't gather on food or dung or dead flesh, but in August they come inside to die by the hundreds. Since Donna has neither swept nor vacuumed, crunchy black mounds are growing all over the house. The windowsill above my head is covered with them, and they're hanging in balls of dust from Joe's long-haired tail.

Penny Dalton and I used to collect piles of clusterflies, then with tweezers we would separate out the intact wings, lick each others wrists and glue them onto each other like jewels. In the summer, some girls plucked the lamps from fireflies and stuck them on their fingers like rings, but not Penny and me. We were fond of fireflies, and would never harm one, for surely such radical surgery would hurt.

"PUT THAT WALKER IN THE CLOSET, Donna," I said yesterday. "I'm tired of looking at it."

"Okay by me," she said. "You won't need it when you break your hip."

I didn't tell her this, but the last thing I'll do is break my hip. If you live in dairy country as long as I have, you ingest enough calcium to keep your bones as strong as barn beams.

I did say, "And don't smoke in this house anymore or I'll ask for someone else."

"You're running out of people," she barked, putting the cigarette out in a saucer.

If I keep feeling this good, I won't need anything from the Social Services. They can keep their walkers and their nastygirl workers who don't even try to read my journal. They can just keep them all down there in Wichner, where the lights stay on all night long just like New York City, and their useless, flowering crabapples are planted in careful pretty rows along the streets, and the sheriff puts someone in jail nearly every week.

They've even opened some kind of supermall just outside of town; a place where everything they sell is made by foreign laborers who work for pennies a day. You'll never see me in a place like that, not until every last locally owned store in town is boarded up and empty.

Reverend Thorne called me this morning. "I won't be coming out to see you until tomorrow, Miss Irene. Do you want me to bring anything?" he asked.

"You sound so far away, Reverend. Where are you?" I replied, making small talk, because Joe did need some dog food and I was out of oatmeal.

"I'm at the mall right now, and I have some business to tend to here in Wichner," he said, then he laughed mysteriously. "I think I'll have a little present for you."

I thought, now what in the world is some holy roller preacher from Wichner going to give me? I should have him come out here and get down on his hands and knees and fetch my notebook out from under the bed, that's what I should do. But I was polite and just asked him to pick up the dogfood and oatmeal. He said he'd be glad to, and that he'd see me soon. Then he laughed in that strange way again and we hung up.

Chapter Thirty

THE FARM LIVES IN THESE NOTEBOOKS, which are tucked away in the simple gun cabinet built without craftsmanship and under duress by my Uncle Alton. It started as a pie safe, a Christmas gift to Mother, but apparently my uncle's command of dimensions was insufficient and the project ended up as a gun cabinet for my father.

Thirty or so of my notebooks are piled neatly on the ammunition shelf. Some of the lined pages show gritty fingerprints, a sign of a rushed entry. A few are splashed with brown stains, blood smeared across the page as I detailed a difficult lambing or made note of a slaughter. Some of my favorite photos are clipped to the brittle pages — mostly photos of animals, startled deer standing in the front yard, various border collies rounding up sheep, a few pictures of owls or close-ups of flowers.

If you wonder when the geese flew south in 1964, I can tell you that, and when they came home again for the summer, I can tell you that too, for this is the kind of information I've spent a third of my life recording. Sometimes I scribbled non sequiturs in the margins: "Geese in a vee flee winter in fall" or "The morning light approaches like God through the window and without warning."

This morning Jim Sinclair came, he said, "Just to say howdy." A person would be dumber than a box of rocks not to know that the man really wanted a look at my guns.

His pink jowls hung like a well-fed dog's, but I must admit, he was quick with a smile and did have the courtesy to remove his hat. He — and evidently everyone else in the whole county — is under the impression that I'm moving to Pine Manor. That's erroneous, of course, but I do wish I had a better plan for my future. I must be careful not to panic, for this end of my life has become untidy.

I said to Sinclair, "What would you want with these old guns?"

"Why, they're antiques, Miss Leahy," he said, as if I didn't know that. "I collect antique guns and buy and sell used fire arms." He smiled self-consciously. I noticed he still wore his wedding band, even though his wife died long ago.

"It's just a little hobby I started when I moved up here. Turned out to be pretty lucrative, too. I'll offer you the highest prices on the contents of your cabinet. I'll even take the cabinet off your hands."

Appreciatively, he stroked the smooth pine boards, studied the square-headed nails, opened the doors. My notebooks were still neatly stacked, waiting. I realized when I saw them, that I had been the last person to touch the pile, that Esther never read one word.

No one has.

And then, as he closed the cabinet doors, for the first time since I was a young girl, I heard the violin. It was as faint as the rustle of lace curtains at an open window, but unmistakable. I shook the sound out of my head like a dog shaking rainwater and knocked myself off-balance. Startled, Sinclair flung his arm in front of me. When I was steady, he sat with me at the kitchen table. I could tell he had heard nothing.

"You've got to watch out for yourself, Miss Leahy," he said. "You gave me quite a scare."

"Nothing to worry about," I said a mite stiffly. "I haven't broken any bones yet, and Donna is usually hereabouts." I had no idea where Donna was, however, and admit that the incident rattled me, especially occurring as it did in front of this particular person.

Perhaps I imagined the music; it had been so soft and had lasted only seconds. Without thinking, I blurted a question that had been on my mind for years. "Mr. Sinclair, why did you run over that cat? The one in front of my house, must be ten years ago or so?"

His confusion was genuine. "You mean on purpose? Why would I do something like that? Now, if it was a snapper I sure would have. Those buggers are too mean to live. But I don't recall killing a cat."

All this time, I have harbored an intense dislike for Jim Sinclair. Now I understand that he either doesn't remember the act that caused my hostility, or my eyes deceived me. This single deed defined him as far as I was concerned, and I'm pressed to wonder how many other senseless acts he's forgotten, or I've misinterpreted.

Sinclair can have my guns; I don't care who gets my possessions. What no one can own, and men like McFee and Mr. Red Ruby cannot sell, is this farm, for although my name is on the deed and the Leahy family is buried on the hill, and drops of our blood have hung like dew on its bedstraw and poverty grass, even I cannot claim possession of this land. Like the sky and air, like the spirit of a child, the earth cannot be owned. Peel back the black asphalt roads, strip away the buildings, expose the ground to sunlight and rain, and green leaves will struggle to the surface.

I just wish I had made a better plan for myself.

REVEREND THORNE WAS SMILING THE SMILE of a man overly pleased with himself when he put the bag on my kitchen table. "Dog food and oatmeal for you, Miss Irene," he said. "Can't visit with you this afternoon, though. I've got a funeral in Wichner."

For a man on his way to a funeral, the Reverend seemed unusually peppy. His eyes were sparkly, like my father's, and clear — barometric eyes, the kind that change from gray to green when the sun is coming out. I do like that in a man.

"Well, thank you, Reverend," I said. I'd hoped to chat with him about Esther, perhaps steer the conversation to this morning's talk with Sinclair and the violin music I think I heard. But he just rushed in and out, dropping the bag of groceries on the kitchen table, along with a big brown envelope. He pointed to it, and said, "I've got to hustle, Miss Irene, but be sure to take a look at these papers."

An urgency spiked with joy filled his voice and immediately my curiosity was piqued. Whatever was in the envelope was the special gift he'd told me about on the telephone the day before, and my hands were shaking as I slit it open. Since Esther left, no one has given me any presents.

I took out several sheets of paper and unfolded them slowly. My teeth turned to chips of ice in my mouth. I read the bold letters on the first page to myself, then out loud:

TO: Irene Constantine Leahy
FROM: The Carniff County Preservation League
RE: A Proposal to Donate Your Property to Carniff County, New York, for Purposes of Establishing a Living-Farm Museum

I hurried as fast as I could to the back door, just in time to see the tail of Reverend Thorne's Subaru disappear over the hill toward Wichner. Thick, dry dust hovered above Pike Road in an ethereal ribbon, then gradually thinned, vanishing altogether as it spread across the fields, across the old apple orchard where branches of the trees stubbornly stretched to the sky.

I read the papers once, twice, three times, and laughed like a child on Christmas morning. My farm, a museum. The first of its kind in Carniff County history. The young Reverend apparently had developed the proposal himself, presented it to the county legislature and gained funding from the Carniff County Preservation League. All I needed to do was sign these papers before a witness, but Donna was nowhere to be seen.

"Donna," I called. "Donna, come here." I called and called, but she did not come.

I sat down at the kitchen table, and Joe limped from behind the stove and rested his head on my knee. I stroked him, thinking about Molly who lives through her many offspring, and of the colt named Patience who introduced me to love and betrayal.

"Donna," I called.

And I thought of Gypsy and Pat, of how they trudged along with Uncle Alton, pulling the plow, or the spreader, or the cutter, while I snuggled in thick wool blankets on the way to school.

"Donna!"

I thought of my sweet Esther who cared for me in every sense, who, Reverend Thorne told me, wears my engagement ring on a chain around her neck. How do you know, I asked, and he said he went to Atlanta to see her, and I nodded at the symmetry.

"Donna?"

"What in Sam Hill are you bellering about, Irene? I'm busy hanging up your laundry. I want to get out of here before five."

But even Donna's imperfections became meaningless, for she witnessed my signature without interest and hurriedly signed her own name to the papers. I put them in the stamped envelope Reverend Thorne had supplied, and smiled as I hung my cane over my arm and followed Joe out the back door.

Sprightly as a disobedient girl, I ignored Donna's protests. The old border collie and I crossed Pike Road and placed the envelope in the mailbox. Reliable Henry Schmidt, the Donohue Flats postman, would pick it up, officially begin the process. I could have clicked my heels.

I LOOK UP THE ROAD, SHADING MY EYES from the sun. The walk to the Leahy cemetery seems short, possible, necessary. I glance back at the house; by now Esther would have come to me, but not Donna, and once again I whisper a thank-you.

Joe, looking brighter than usual, watches me expectantly. Together, I leaning heavily on my wooden cane, Joe gimpy but enthusiastic, we shuffle up the hill. When we get to the top, we are only slightly out of breath.

The cemetery has been prepared to receive guests. Reverend Thorne has straightened the gravestones, the high grass is clipped close to the ground. The names of my family — William, Virginia, Billy, and Alton Leahy — peek from behind wild, late-blooming asters. On each grave an immense begonia wells up from the ground in a splendor of perfect orange.

Joe is prone, panting in the sun and I, my breath shallow, finally collapse, at risk. I lie next to him in the clover, facing the cloud-free sky, thinking of my father and the way he tended his apple trees meditatively, unattached to this world. I think of Mother's complicated, faraway expression as she watched the flock grazing in these very fields. And of my brother Billy who died too early, but guided me, walking this land with me. He has sent his ghostly messages, in the whispers of the breeze and in the scent of newborn lambs and lavender. I have never been alone.

And then the laughter wells at the thought of anyone seeing me in my pale pink nightgown, laid out on the grass among the gravestones. It tickles me to tears. Joe licks my face and I laugh with the joy of a totally free woman.

It is when I sit up to catch my breath and wipe my eyes, that I hear it again — the music — and the final mystery is solved. It is a rattle in the throat perhaps, or a sign of faulty respiration, not a special sound after all, remarkable only because, like my father, I always seem to hear things differently than most.